W9-CLH-655

WE'LL SOON
BE HOME AGAIN

Jessica Bab Bonde

Peter Bergting

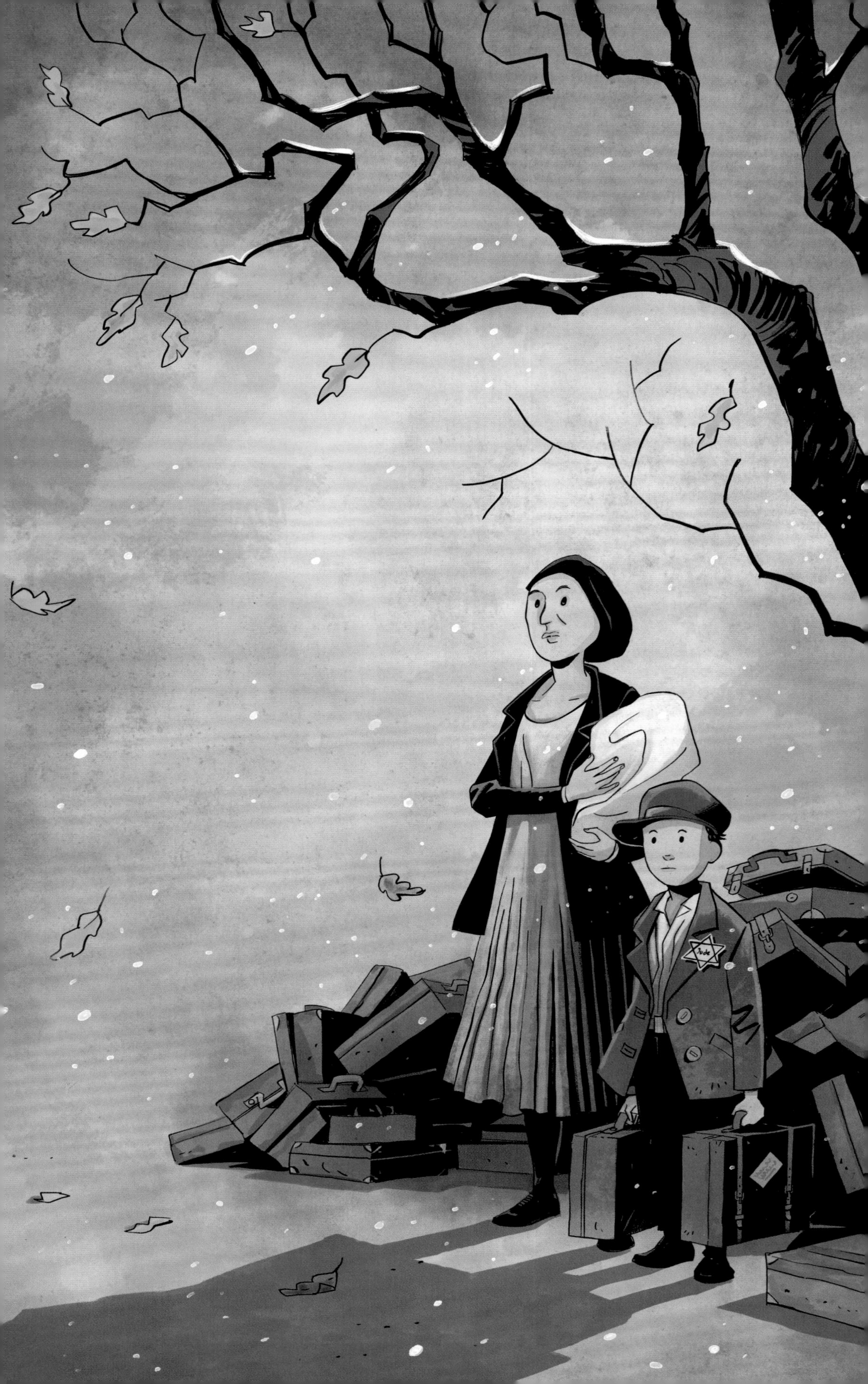
Jude

WE'LL SOON BE HOME AGAIN

Story
Jessica Bab Bonde
Art
Peter Bergting

—

Translation
Jessica Bab Bonde & Sunshine Barbito
Lettering
Kathryn Renta

DARK HORSE BOOKS

To those who have made me who I am and given me the opportunity to live and breathe freely.

—JBB

Editor SCOTT ALLIE
Assistant Editor SUNSHINE BARBITO
Designers RICK DeLUCCO and JUSTIN COUCH
Digital Art Technician ALLYSON HALLER
Special thanks to Michael Gombos, Catharina Lantz, and David Campiti

Mike Richardson *President and Publisher* Neil Hankerson *Executive Vice President* Tom Weddle *Chief Financial Officer* Randy Stradley *Vice President of Publishing* Nick McWhorter *Chief Business Development Officer* Dale LaFountain *Chief Information Officer* Matt Parkinson *Vice President of Marketing* Cara Niece *Vice President of Production and Scheduling* Mark Bernardi *Vice President of Book Trade and Digital Sales* Ken Lizzi *General Counsel* Dave Marshall *Editor in Chief* Davey Estrada *Editorial Director* Chris Warner *Senior Books Editor* Cary Grazzini *Director of Specialty Projects* Lia Ribacchi *Art Director* Vanessa Todd-Holmes *Director of Print Purchasing* Matt Dryer *Director of Digital Art and Prepress* Michael Gombos *Senior Director of Licensed Publications* Kari Yadro *Director of Custom Programs* Kari Torson *Director of International Licensing* Sean Brice *Director of Trade Sales*

Originally published in Sweden by Natur & Kultur, 2018

Published by Dark Horse Books, a division of Dark Horse Comics LLC
10956 SE Main Street Milwaukie, OR 97222

DarkHorse.com
Advertising Sales: (503) 905-2315
Comic Shop Locator Service: Comicshoplocator.com

10 9 8 7 6 5 4 3 2 1

Printed in China

We'll Soon Be Home Again, March 2020. Published by Dark Horse Comics LLC, 10956 SE Main Street, Milwaukie, Oregon 97222. We'll Soon Be Home Again text copyright © 2018, 2020 Jessica Bab Bonde, art copyright © 2018, 2020 Peter Bergting. Dark Horse Books® and the Dark Horse logo are trademarks of Dark Horse Comics LLC, registered in various categories and countries. All rights reserved. No portion of this publication may be reproduced or transmitted, in any form or by any means, without the express written permission of Dark Horse Comics LLC. Names, characters, places, and incidents featured in this publication either are the product of the author's imagination or are used fictitiously. Any resemblance to actual persons (living or dead), events, institutions, or locales, without satiric intent, is coincidental.

Library of Congress Cataloging-in-Publication Data

Names: Bab Bonde, Jessica, author. | Bergting, Peter, artist. | Barbito, Sunshine, translator. | Renta, Kathryn S., letterer.
Title: We'll soon be home again / story, Jessica Bab Bonde ; art, Peter Bergting ; translation, Jessica Bab Bonde & Sunshine Barbito ; letterer, Kathryn Renta.
Other titles: Vi kommer snart hem igen. English | We will soon be home again
Description: Milwaukie, OR : Dark Horse Books, 2020. | Audience: Ages 12+ | Audience: Grades 7-9 | Summary: Based on interviews with six Holocaust survivors, these first-person point of view stories relate living through the de-humanization and starvation in concentration camps and the industrial-scale mass murder in extermination camps.
Identifiers: LCCN 2019043599 (print) | LCCN 2019043600 (ebook) | ISBN 9781506715490 (paperback) | ISBN 9781506715667 (ebook)
Subjects: LCSH: Graphic novels. | CYAC: Graphic novels. | Holocaust, Jewish (1939-1945)--Fiction. | Survival--Fiction.
Classification: LCC PZ7.7.B157 We 2020 (print) | LCC PZ7.7.B157 (ebook) | DDC 741.5/9485--dc23
LC record available at https://lccn.loc.gov/2019043599
LC ebook record available at https://lccn.loc.gov/2019043600

TABLE OF CONTENTS

FOREWORD

Tobias, Livia, Selma, Susanna, Emerich, and Elisabeth. Their lives started just like mine or yours. It's possible they were even more lucky than you are. They were all born into safety and comfort with family and friends around. They had homes, they had food and clothes. They had the same thoughts and troubles that all children do. They had freedom and were able to grow, play with friends, and some of them would start school, others would even start university. Not any happier or any sadder than other children. They lived just like you and I do.

Then, suddenly, their lives started to change. For some, the change was slow. So slow that they hardly noticed it. They weren't allowed on certain streets, couldn't play with children in the parks, and maybe had to quit school. For some, it all happened overnight. They were forced to move to other parts of their cities and to live squeezed in together with people they didn't know. They couldn't work or go to school. They had no money and hardly any food. Soon, all joy, comfort, and everyday life was taken from them. Soon there was only fear and fighting for their lives.

All of them lost parents, siblings, best friends, homes, clothes, favorite things. More or less, their whole lives. How could that happen? Could that happen to us? To you and me?

While all of this happened, life went on like usual for many people, as though nothing had happened at all. Some of them would protest. They'd speak out about what they found strange or wrong. For example, that their friends, colleagues, and classmates were no longer allowed to work or study simply because they were Jewish. Simply because, in one way or another, they deviated from what the rulers claimed was "normal." But there weren't enough who took a stand. Too many didn't care, too many did not sympathize with the ones being exposed. Too many looked the other way and were happy as long as nothing happened to them or their families.

I believe that these things can happen to us, to you and me and to our families. In other places around the world, but also here in our country. Unfortunately, I believe it could happen easily. It can happen when we stop caring about how we treat each other, about what's okay and what's not okay to do.

Tobias, Livia, Selma, Susanna, Emerich, and Elisabeth have told us about their lives, so that you will get the chance to understand what can happen if we are not careful with the freedom that we have today. We cannot take the right to live freely for granted. If we are to think freely as we choose to, we must also let others think and believe as they want to. Sometimes it's difficult to accept that another's beliefs may be different from ours, even challenging to ours. But we must live side by side. Sometimes that might seem like a bad idea. But to coexist peacefully is much better than having someone take your freedoms away, to violate your human rights, because of your own beliefs. You and me and our friends, we are all responsible for our world, and how we want it to be. We have to share that responsibility. Together.

Jessica Bab Bonde

**Stockholm, Sweden
October 2017**

GHETTO I LODZ

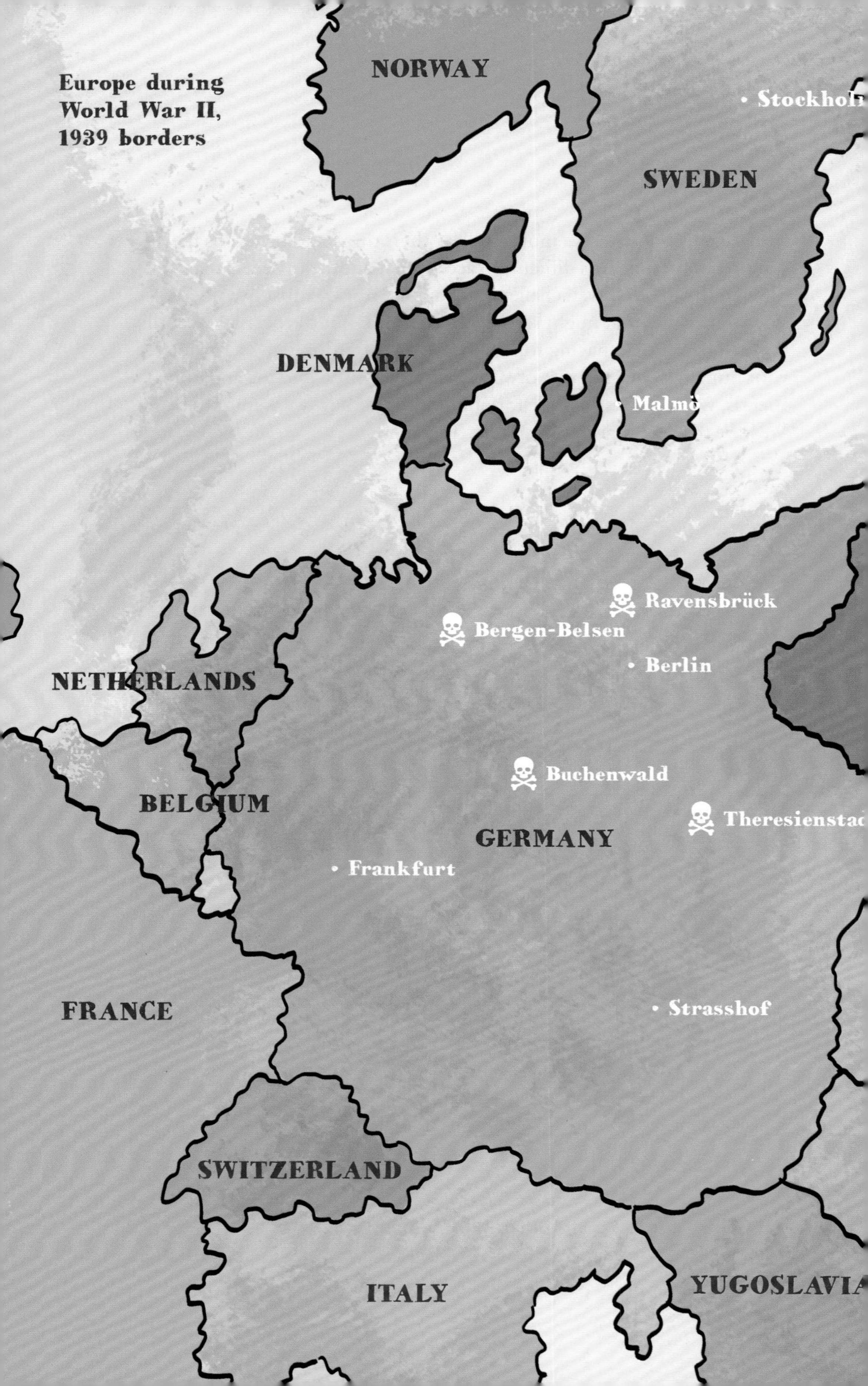

Europe during World War II, 1939 borders
NORWAY
Stockholm
SWEDEN
DENMARK
Malmö
Ravensbrück
Bergen-Belsen
Berlin
NETHERLANDS
Buchenwald
BELGIUM
Theresienstadt
GERMANY
Frankfurt
FRANCE
Strasshof
SWITZERLAND
ITALY
YUGOSLAVIA

MY MOTHER'S NAME WAS ESTER.

MUM AND DAD HAD A GROCERY STORE IN LODZ. THE STORE WAS ALL WE HAD.

Tobias

IN THE SUMMERS, MY MUM AND I WOULD GO UP TO THE MOUNTAINS, TO ZAKOPANE.

RAWET

IN ZAKOPANE, THERE WAS FRESH AIR AND WE COULD REST. WHILE WE WERE GONE, DAD TOOK CARE OF THE STORE.

IN THE AUTUMN OF 1939, LODZ BECAME A GERMAN CITY.

THE MAIN STREET'S NAME CHANGED TO HITLERSTRASE. THE GERMANS THOUGHT THAT ALL JEWS IN LODZ SHOULD LIVE IN THE SAME AREA.

THAT AREA WAS CALLED THE GHETTO.

FROM THEN ON, THE JEWS WERE NOT ALLOWED TO WALK ON HITLERSTRASE.

MY FAMILY WAS FORCED TO MOVE INTO AN OLD THREE-BEDROOM APARTMENT IN THE GHETTO.

MUM, DAD, AND I STAYED IN THE LIVING ROOM. MY FATHER'S MOTHER STAYED IN A SCRUB CORNER, AND MY DAD'S TWO BROTHERS SHARED ONE ROOM.

IN THE GHETTO, MANY ORPHANS LIVED ON THE STREET. THEIR PARENTS HAD BEEN TAKEN IN DIFFERENT RAIDS. ONE DAY, THEY NEVER CAME HOME FROM WORK.

SOON THERE WERE MORE AND MORE OF THEM. I REMEMBER THEIR GREY CHEEKS, AND THEIR EYES SUNKEN INTO THEIR FACES.

AS TIME PASSED, THEY ALL DISAPPEARED, ONE BY ONE.

EVERY TENTH DAY WE FETCHED OUR BREAD RATION.

IS THIS *ALL* WE GET? HOW ARE WE SUPPOSED TO LIVE ON THIS?

I REMEMBER MY MUM SWEEPING THE BREAD INTO DAMP CLOTHS. EVERY MORNING SHE WOULD CUT IT INTO THIN SLICES AND DIVIDE IT BETWEEN THE SIX OF US.

GOOD, IT HAS NOT MOLDED YET.

MY GRANDMOTHER DIED FROM MALNUTRITION DURING PASSOVER.

MY GRANDMOTHER WAS LUCKY. SHE GOT TO DIE WHEN ALL OF US WERE STILL TOGETHER.

BY THE END OF AUGUST 1942, ALL CHILDREN UNDER TEN WERE SUPPOSED TO BE HANDED OVER.

TOLEK, COME QUICKLY!

TRUCKS DROVE INTO THE GHETTO AND TOOK ALL OF THE SICK PEOPLE FROM THE HOSPITALS. THEY WENT FROM HOUSE TO HOUSE AND TOOK ALL OF THE ELDERLY PEOPLE, EVERYONE UNABLE TO WORK, AND ALL CHILDREN UNDER TEN YEARS OLD.

THEY WERE THROWN ONTO THE FLATBEDS.

TOLEK, SIT ON THE MATTRESS. YOU CAN LAY DOWN, STAND UP, OR SIT. BUT YOU CANNOT LEAVE THE MATTRESS, AND YOU *CANNOT* MAKE ANY NOISE.

MY MUM AND DAD VISITED EVERY EVENING TO BRING ME FOOD AND WATER. WHEN THEY LEFT, THEY TOOK THE BUCKET THAT I USED AS A TOILET DURING THE DAY.

I SAT ALONE IN THE ATTIC FOR ONE MONTH AND TWENTY DAYS.

ONE DAY MUM AND DAD TOLD ME I COULD COME BACK DOWN WITH THEM.

I WAS ACTUALLY SIX YEARS OLD, BUT MY PARENTS HAD ARRANGED PAPERS FOR ME CLAIMING THAT I WAS TEN.

THIS MEANT I COULD WORK AND WAS ENTITLED TO RATIONING CARDS. I BECAME AN APPRENTICE IN THE FACTORY WHERE MY DAD WORKED.

I WAS ALIVE. I HAD SURVIVED. I WAS WORKING IN THE GHETTO.

TRANSPORT AFTER TRANSPORT LEFT, MOSTLY FOR AUSCHWITZ. BUT NO ONE HAD A CLUE WHAT WAS GOING ON THERE.

ONE CHILD IN ONE THOUSAND SURVIVED THE GHETTO IN LODZ AND THE TIME THEREAFTER. I WAS ONE OF THE CHILDREN THAT SURVIVED.

I OFTEN THINK OF HOW LUCKY I AM.

IN THE GHETTO, THERE WAS AN OFFICER. FRANZ SEIFFERT. BY THE AUTUMN OF 1944, HE REALIZED THAT THE GERMANS WERE LOSING THE WAR ...

...AND HE WANTED TO GET AWAY AS SOON AS POSSIBLE.

HE CREATED A PROJECT TO TAKE HIM OUT OF THE GHETTO. AND US, TOO, AS IT WOULD TURN OUT.

HE WOULD HELP TO REBUILD WAR-DAMAGED GERMANY. FOR THIS HE NEEDED THREE HUNDRED PRISONERS, WHICH HE HIMSELF PICKED OUT.

ONE OF THEM WAS MY DAD--FOR WHAT REASON, I DO NOT KNOW.

MY DAD AND HIS CLOSEST FAMILY WERE TO LEAVE THE GHETTO.

16

BY THE END OF OCTOBER, IT WAS TIME.

I REMEMBER THE TWO TRAINS WAITING AT THE STATION.

MY DAD AND THE OTHER PRISONERS GOT ON ONE TRAIN. WHEN ALL THREE HUNDRED HAD EMBARKED, THE TRAIN LEFT THE STATION.

AFTER THAT, IT WAS TIME FOR MUM AND THE REST OF US TO GO. WE WERE STOWED WITH THE OTHER WOMEN AND CHILDREN IN THE TRAIN CAR IN THE MOST AWFUL WAY ONE CAN IMAGINE.

AT ONE END OF THE WAGON WAS A BUCKET OF WATER, AND AT THE OTHER AN EMPTY BUCKET. THE LATTER WOULD SERVE AS OUR TOILET.

I TRIED TO FIND A SMALL OPENING BETWEEN THE BOARDS TO BREATHE SOME FRESH AIR.

SUDDENLY, ONE DAY, THE TRAIN STOPPED.

THE HEAVY DOORS OPENED AND WE COULD FINALLY BREATHE SOME FRESH AIR. A BLESSING.

WE HAD ARRIVED TO RAVENSBRÜCK--A WOMEN'S CONCENTRATION CAMP WHERE WE WERE KEPT WHILE WAITING FOR MR. SEIFFERT'S PROJECT TO BE READY, SO THAT WE COULD START WORKING THERE.

OUT! OUT!

WOOF

WOOF

NO ONE KNEW HOW LONG WE WOULD STAY.

WOOF WOOF

WOOF

GET UNDRESSED BY THE WALL!

OUR MOTHERS WERE FORCED TO TAKE OFF THEIR CLOTHES.

NOT THE CHILDREN!

WE WERE TRANSFORMED INTO SOMETHING ELSE. SOMETHING FAR FROM HUMAN.

SOMETHING EASIER TO MURDER.

WE WERE EACH GIVEN A NUMBER.

I WAS NO LONGER A HUMAN BEING. I WAS A NUMBER.

79295.

RAVENSBRÜCK COULD "HOUSE" THIRTY THOUSAND PEOPLE.

WHERE WERE ALL THE OTHERS, THE ONES BEFORE ME?

WHILE HAVING OUR PRISONER NUMBERS ASSIGNED WE WERE GIVEN ONE POSSESSION--A CUP.

AFTER THAT, I WALKED TO MY NEW HOME-- BARRACKS TWENTY-TWO.

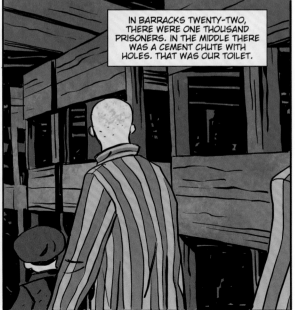

IN BARRACKS TWENTY-TWO, THERE WERE ONE THOUSAND PRISONERS. IN THE MIDDLE THERE WAS A CEMENT CHUTE WITH HOLES. THAT WAS OUR TOILET.

MUM AND I GOT A BED ON TOP. WE HAD TO CLIMB THE POST OF THE BED TO GET UP.

WE HAD TO SLEEP FEET TO FEET WITH ANOTHER BOY AND HIS MUM.

IN THE MORNING, COFFEE WAS HANDED OUT--LUKEWARM WATER WITH BARK.

AFTER THAT, WE STOOD OUTSIDE WAITING TO BE COUNTED.

IT WAS NEVER THE SAME AS THE DAY BEFORE.

AT SIX O'CLOCK, WHEN THE COUNTING WAS DONE, THE DOORS TO OUR BARRACKS WERE LOCKED.

WE WENT TO WORK. ME AND MY MUM WORKED OUT IN THE WOODS.

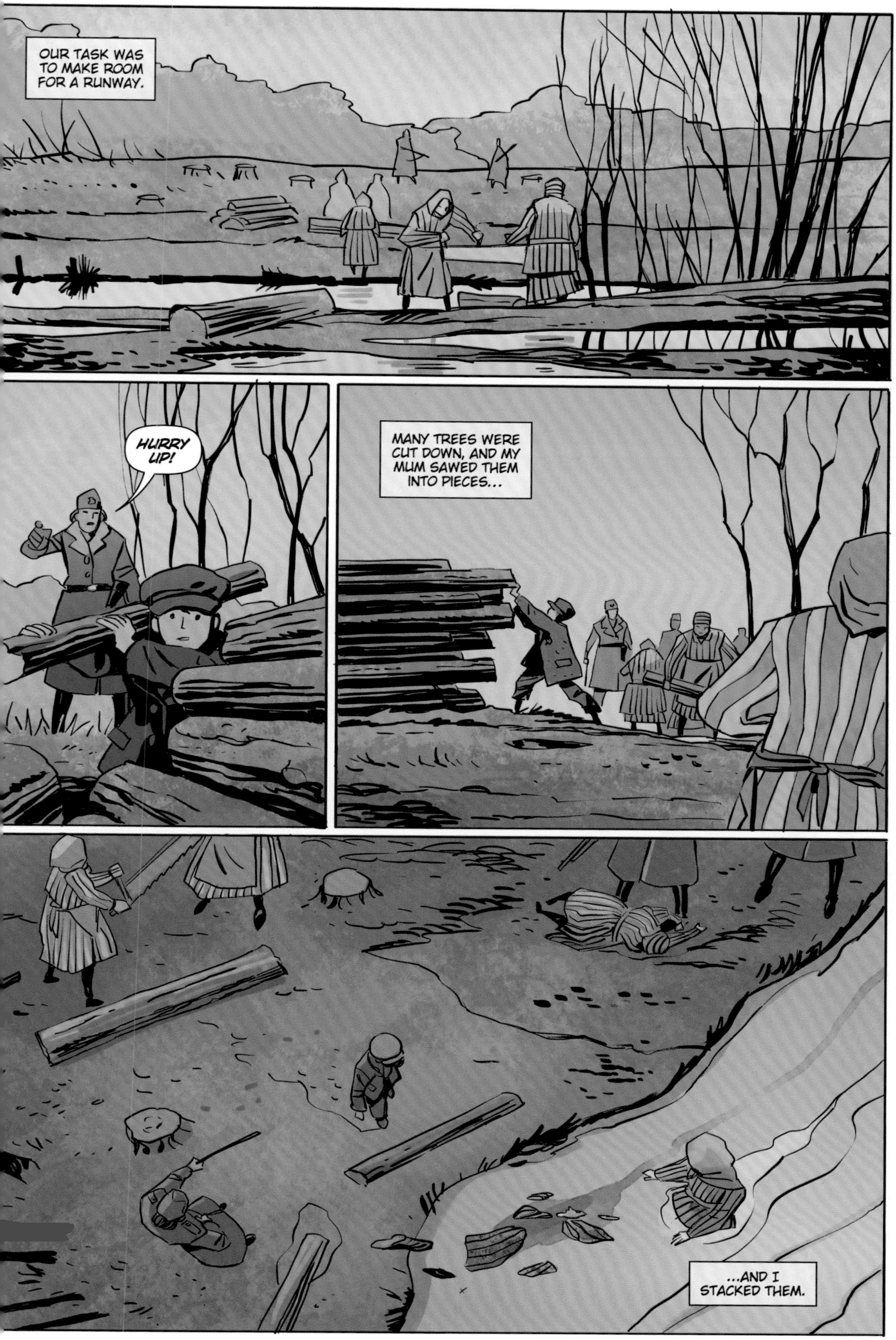
OUR TASK WAS TO MAKE ROOM FOR A RUNWAY.
HURRY UP!
MANY TREES WERE CUT DOWN, AND MY MUM SAWED THEM INTO PIECES...
...AND I STACKED THEM.

FOR LUNCH WE HAD A PIECE OF SAUSAGE AND SOME SOUP MADE OF WATER AND POTATO SKIN.

EVERY DAY MY MUM GAVE ME HER PIECE OF SAUSAGE. SHE WANTED ME TO SURVIVE.

OUR TIME SPENT IN THE GHETTO WAS AWFUL, BUT BEING IN RAVENSBRÜCK WAS HELL. I HAD MY MUM, THOUGH, AND FOR THAT I WAS LUCKY.

AND IT WAS A CONCENTRATION CAMP, NOT AN EXTERMINATION CAMP. IF WE HAD BEEN SENT TO AN EXTERMINATION CAMP WE WOULD HAVE BEEN KILLED IMMEDIATELY.

THEY DID THAT TO EVERYONE TOO WEAK, TOO YOUNG, OR TOO OLD.

OUTSIDE BERLIN.

WHEN THE FACTORY WAS BUILT, FRANZ SEIFFERT SENT FOR HIS PRISONERS. WE WENT BY TRAIN TO A NEW PLACE WHERE WE WOULD CONTINUE TO FIGHT FOR OUR LIVES.

WE WORKED ALL THROUGH THE DAYS, FROM EARLY MORNING TO SUNSET. WE WERE HUNTED AND BEATEN AS IN RAVENSBRÜCK. AND WE STARVED, JUST AS BEFORE.

WHAT'S HAPPENING?

QUICK! TO THE SHELTERS!

WE HID FOR MANY DAYS. ONE MORNING, EVERYTHING WAS QUIET.

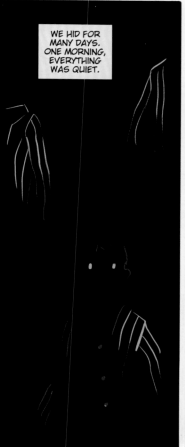

THE GATES TO THE CAMP WERE OPENED BY THE RUSSIAN ARMY. THEY TOLD US THE WAR WAS OVER. WE WERE FREE.

THE HUNGER DROVE US, THOUGH WE WERE WEAK. AND WE FOUND MY DAD.

WE RETURNED TO LODZ, OUR OLD HOMETOWN, AND REOPENED OUR GROCERY STORE.

WE FOUND A NEW HOUSE TO LIVE IN. OTHER PEOPLE WERE LIVING IN OUR OLD HOUSE.

MY PARENTS SPENT ALL THEIR TIME LOOKING FOR OUR LOVED ONES. MY DAD FOUND OUT THAT HIS YOUNGER BROTHER HAD ARRIVED IN SWEDEN WITH THE RED CROSS *WHITE BUSES*.

BY THE FALL OF 1945, I STARTED TO GO TO SCHOOL. I WAS NINE YEARS OLD AND HAD NEVER BEEN. I DIDN'T KNOW HOW TO READ OR WRITE.

LESS THAN ONE YEAR LATER, FORTY-THREE JEWS WERE KILLED BY POLICE, MILITARY, AND CIVILIANS IN THE TOWN OF KIELCE. THIS IS KNOWN AS THE KIELCE MASSACRE.

JEWS WERE HUNTED AND BEATEN IN POLAND. AGAIN.

MY DAD MISSED HIS BROTHER.

AFTER MANY BRIBES AND STRUGGLES, WE GOT PASSPORTS TO TRAVEL TO SWEDEN.

I WAS TWELVE YEARS OLD WHEN OUR TRAIN ARRIVED IN STOCKHOLM CENTRAL STATION. MY UNCLE MET US WITH AN ELDERLY AUNT OF MINE, WHO I HAD NEVER MET BEFORE.

SHE ASKED ME MY NAME. "TOLEK," I ANSWERED.

TOLEK? THAT IS NOT A NAME HERE. YOU MUST HAVE A SWEDISH NAME. CHOOSE BETWEEN TOMMY OR TOBIAS.

I THOUGHT TOBIAS SEEMED NICE, SO THAT WAS MY CHOICE.

MY UNCLE LIVED IN A TWO-ROOM APARTMENT OUTSIDE OF STOCKHOLM.

WE WERE ONLY ALLOWED TO STAY FOR TWO WEEKS.

ONE DAY A NEIGHBOR TOLD US ABOUT THE FOREIGN POLICE. I WAS SENT TO THEM AND THEY SAID, "TOBIAS, THROW YOUR PASSPORTS AWAY. COME HERE, AND I WILL GIVE YOU PROTECTION PASSPORTS."

WE BECAME STATELESS.

BUT WE WERE WELCOME.

AFTER A WHILE I COULD START SCHOOL AGAIN, IN SWEDEN.

I HAD ARRIVED IN PARADISE.

WHEN I WAS TWENTY-FIVE YEARS OLD, I MET MONIKA. WE GOT MARRIED AND MADE A HAPPY HOME FOR US AND OUR THREE CHILDREN.

In 1992, **Tobias Rawet** heard the French historical revisionist Robert Faurisson claim that the Holocaust never happened. He was shocked. His terrible childhood experiences never took place? He decided to devote his life to telling the true story about what can happen when anti-democratic forces are allowed to reign, and to tell the truth about what can happen if everyone's human rights are not defended. Since then, he has called on every young person to open their eyes and to work for equality and tolerance.

Livia

MY NAME IS
LIVIA FRÄNKEL.

I WAS BORN IN SIGHET. THE TOWN
HAS HAD GREAT INFLUENCE ON
EUROPEAN AND JEWISH HISTORY.

THE CITY OF SIGHET SITS IN THE
NORTH OF TRANSYLVANIA WHERE
THE RIVERS TISZA AND IZA MEET
IN A BILLOWY LANDSCAPE,
SURROUNDED BY MOUNTAINS.

THERE WERE FOUR OF US IN MY
FAMILY. ME AND MY OLDER SISTER HÉDI,
MY DAD IGNATZ, AND MY MUM FRIDA. AS
A CHILD I WAS LOVED VERY MUCH.

WHEN I THINK BACK I AM SO
GRATEFUL FOR ALL THE COMFORT,
CARE, AND SAFETY MY SIBLINGS AND I
WERE GIVEN. I BELIEVE THAT ONE CAN
WITHSTAND LIFE'S STRUGGLES MUCH
EASIER WITH A FOUNDATION OF LOVE.

WE WERE A MIDDLE-CLASS JEWISH FAMILY. MY DAD HAD A BUSINESS PRODUCING PACKAGING. MY SISTER AND I HAD EVERYTHING WE NEEDED.

WE LIVED IN A BEAUTIFUL OLD HOUSE IN SIGHET. AFTER A WHILE, WE MOVED TO A NEWLY BUILT HOME.

THE FIRST TIME I EXPERIENCED HARASSMENT BECAUSE OF MY JEWISH HERITAGE WAS WHEN I STARTED SCHOOL.

STINKING, *DISGUSTING JEW!* WHAT ARE YOU DOING HERE WITH US NORMAL PEOPLE?

YOU MAKE THE AIR SMELL BAD. GO BACK TO YOUR *OWN COUNTRY!*

I WAS TERRIFIED. I RAN.

ONE OF THE BOYS CAME AFTER ME AND HE PUSHED ME OVER. I SCRAPED MY KNEE.

DEVASTATED, I RAN TO MY MUM. SHE WAS SITTING AT THE KITCHEN TABLE WHEN I GOT HOME. I LOOKED DESTROYED AND MY KNEE WAS BLEEDING.

WHY ARE THEY SO *MEAN?*

WHICH COUNTRY IS *OUR* COUNTRY? WEREN'T WE *BORN* HERE? OUR FAMILY HAS LIVED HERE FOR GENERATIONS, HAVEN'T WE?

ONE DAY, MY DAD BROUGHT A RADIO HOME WITH HIM. THAT MEANT A LOT FOR US.

MY SISTER AND I THOUGHT IT WAS AMAZING, LISTENING TO MUSIC FROM BERLIN, PARIS, AND LONDON.

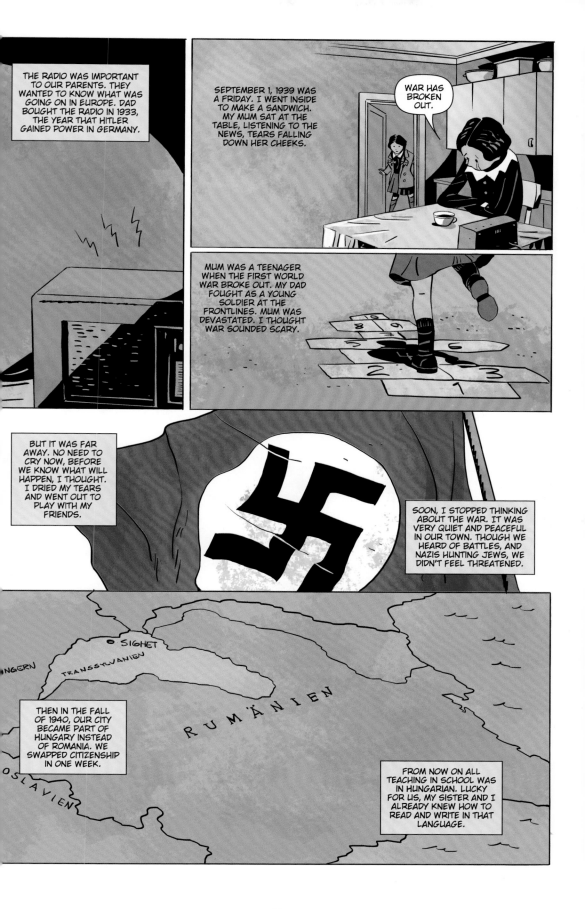

THE RADIO WAS IMPORTANT TO OUR PARENTS. THEY WANTED TO KNOW WHAT WAS GOING ON IN EUROPE. DAD BOUGHT THE RADIO IN 1933, THE YEAR THAT HITLER GAINED POWER IN GERMANY.

SEPTEMBER 1, 1939 WAS A FRIDAY. I WENT INSIDE TO MAKE A SANDWICH. MY MUM SAT AT THE TABLE, LISTENING TO THE NEWS, TEARS FALLING DOWN HER CHEEKS.

WAR HAS BROKEN OUT.

MUM WAS A TEENAGER WHEN THE FIRST WORLD WAR BROKE OUT. MY DAD FOUGHT AS A YOUNG SOLDIER AT THE FRONTLINES. MUM WAS DEVASTATED. I THOUGHT WAR SOUNDED SCARY.

BUT IT WAS FAR AWAY. NO NEED TO CRY NOW, BEFORE WE KNOW WHAT WILL HAPPEN, I THOUGHT. I DRIED MY TEARS AND WENT OUT TO PLAY WITH MY FRIENDS.

SOON, I STOPPED THINKING ABOUT THE WAR. IT WAS VERY QUIET AND PEACEFUL IN OUR TOWN. THOUGH WE HEARD OF BATTLES, AND NAZIS HUNTING JEWS, WE DIDN'T FEEL THREATENED.

SIGHET

NGERN

TRANSSYLVANIEN

RUMÄNIEN

OSLAVIEN

THEN IN THE FALL OF 1940, OUR CITY BECAME PART OF HUNGARY INSTEAD OF ROMANIA. WE SWAPPED CITIZENSHIP IN ONE WEEK.

FROM NOW ON ALL TEACHING IN SCHOOL WAS IN HUNGARIAN. LUCKY FOR US, MY SISTER AND I ALREADY KNEW HOW TO READ AND WRITE IN THAT LANGUAGE.

OUR LIVES STARTED TO CHANGE. A NEW LAW FORBID NON-JEWS TO SHOP IN STORES OWNED BY JEWS.

AS LONG AS WE ARE TOGETHER, WE ARE SAFE.

WITH FEWER CUSTOMERS IN OUR SHOP, WE FELL ON ROUGH TIMES.

THEN THE HUNGARIAN GOVERNMENT TOOK OUR BELONGINGS. WE WERE NOT ALLOWED TO HAVE MONEY IN THE BANK, OR OWN JEWELRY, ART, OR CARPETS. WE COULD NOT HAVE ANY VEHICLES, CARS, OR HORSE CARRIAGES.

ALL THROUGH MY CHILDHOOD I HAD LONGED FOR A BICYCLE, BUT I HAD HAD TO WAIT BECAUSE IT WAS SO EXPENSIVE. FINALLY ON MY BIRTHDAY THE YEAR BEFORE THE LAW WAS INTRODUCED, I HAD GOTTEN MY RED BICYCLE.

NOW I WAS FORCED TO HAND IT TO THE AUTHORITIES. WE ALSO HANDED IN OUR RADIO. SLOWLY THINGS CHANGED, BUT WE TRIED TO KEEP OUR LIVES AS NORMAL AS WE COULD. ALL THE WHILE, WE HOPED FOR THE WAR TO END.

IN 1942, JEWS WERE NO LONGER ALLOWED TO GO TO HIGH SCHOOL. TO ME THAT WAS THE TOUGHEST CHANGE. MY SISTER HAD ONE YEAR LEFT UNTIL HER GRADUATION, AND I WAS JUST ABOUT TO START.

IN LARGER CITIES, THERE WERE JEWISH SCHOOLS, BUT THESE SCHOOLS WERE FAR WAY. WE HAD TO STAY WITH OTHER FAMILIES.

OUR SCHOOL WAS IN THE CAPITAL OF TRANSYLVANIA, CLUJ. IT WAS FAR FROM HOME AND TRAVELING WAS EXPENSIVE. WE COULD ONLY COME HOME FOR THE HIGH HOLIDAYS AND SCHOOL BREAKS.

IT WAS HARD BEING SO FAR AWAY FROM MUM AND DAD.

SIGHET IS SITUATED BY THE BORDER WITH UKRAINE. IN 1943 WHEN I GOT HOME FOR WINTER BREAK, THERE WERE A LOT OF RUMORS SAYING THE RUSSIANS WERE CLOSE. IF THE RUSSIANS CAME THE WAR WOULD BE OVER.

MY DAD THOUGHT THINGS COULD GET CHAOTIC SO HE ASKED ME TO STAY HOME AND NOT GO BACK TO SCHOOL UNTIL THINGS CALMED DOWN.

HE SAID THE MOST IMPORTANT THING WAS FOR US TO BE TOGETHER. THAT SOUNDED OKAY TO ME.

I HAD MY BOOKS AND COULD KEEP UP WITH MY STUDIES FROM HOME. IF THE RUSSIANS ARRIVED AND THE WAR ENDED, MY LIFE COULD CONTINUE AS BEFORE.

MANY OF MY FRIENDS STUDIED IN OTHER PARTS OF THE COUNTRY. WE HADN'T SEEN EACH OTHER FOR A LONG TIME AND WERE ALL BACK IN SIGHET FOR WINTER BREAK. WE DECIDED TO CELEBRATE NEW YEAR'S EVE AT A GIRLFRIEND'S HOUSE WHOSE PARENTS WERE AWAY. WE COOKED A NICE MEAL AND LISTENED TO THE LATEST JAZZ.

WE SAT AROUND THE TABLE AND TOLD EACH OTHER OUR DREAMS FOR THE FUTURE, TAKING TURNS TALKING ABOUT OUR PLANS FOR WHEN THE WAR WAS OVER.

WE WERE CONVINCED WE'D MEET AGAIN IN THE COMING YEAR, 1945, WHEN WE'D FINALLY BE FREE. WE'D MEET AGAIN AND TELL EACH OTHER ABOUT WHAT WE HAD DONE DURING THE YEAR THAT HAD PASSED.

BUT THAT NEVER HAPPENED.

THE NEW YEAR CAME. I WAS HOME IN SIGHET WAITING FOR THE RUSSIANS. INSTEAD, ONE DAY, GERMAN SOLDIERS CAME DOWN THE STREETS. FOR THE FIRST TIME I FEARED FOR OUR LIVES.

WHEN THE AUTHORITIES GAVE US INFORMATION, THEY DID IT AS IN THE OLDEN DAYS--THEY'D SEND A MESSENGER BOY WITH A DRUM.

HE ANNOUNCED THAT FROM NOW ON JEWS WOULD WEAR THE YELLOW STAR OF DAVID ATTACHED TO OUR COATS ABOVE OUR HEARTS.

DON'T WORRY. WE ARE NOT ASHAMED OF BEING JEWS.

TWO WEEKS LATER WE HEARD THE DRUMMER BOY AGAIN. WE WERE TO MOVE TO THE OUTSKIRTS OF THE CITY.

ALL NON-JEWS LIVING THERE WOULD MOVE OUT. AT THE SAME TIME, STREET BY STREET, THE TEN THOUSAND JEWS IN OUR TOWN WOULD LEAVE OUR HOMES.

OUR STREET WAS ONE OF THE FIRST.

WE WERE SHOCKED. IT FELT LIKE SOMEONE HAD HIT US ON THE HEAD. WHY WERE WE FORCED TO LEAVE OUR BEAUTIFUL HOME?

BEFORE WE LEFT, MUM HID SOME MONEY WITH OUR NEIGHBOR MRS. FEKETE. WE WERE AMONG THE FIRST TO BE SENT TO THE GHETTO. AFTER A FEW WEEKS, ALL OF THE MONEY WE'D BROUGHT WAS GONE.

EVERY DAY, GROUPS OF JEWS LEFT TO WORK IN THE CITY. MY SISTER SAID SHE COULD APPLY FOR WORK AND SNEAK AWAY TO MRS. FEKETE.

"I DON'T KNOW WHAT YOU'RE TALKING ABOUT," MRS. FEKETE TOLD HER. HÉDI REPLIED, "THE MONEY MY MUM LEFT FOR YOU BEFORE WE WERE FORCED AWAY." MRS. FEKETE SAID, "DON'T JUST STAND HERE MAKING THINGS UP. GO AWAY NOW OR I'LL CALL THE POLICE."

HÉDI WENT AWAY WITHOUT THE MONEY. MRS. FEKETE KEPT EVERYTHING FOR HERSELF.

AFTER FOUR WEEKS ALL OF THE JEWS IN SIGHET HAD BEEN MOVED. WE HEARD THE SOUND FROM THE DRUMMER AGAIN. BY THEN WE HAD NOTHING LEFT. I THOUGHT, IS IT OUR LIVES THEY WANT?

THE GHETTO WAS TO BE EMPTIED. EVERY PERSON SENT AWAY. AT SIX O'CLOCK THE NEXT MORNING, WE WERE TO BE READY FOR DEPARTURE. I DON'T THINK ANYONE SLEPT THAT NIGHT.

WE PASSED THROUGH OUR TOWN AS EVERYONE BEGAN TO WAKE UP. WE CONTINUED THROUGH THE PARK.

THE SKY WAS CLEAR, TREES AND FLOWERS EVERYWHERE. BIRDS SINGING.

I HAD THIS HORRID FEELING THAT THIS WAS THE LAST TIME I'D SEE MY HOMETOWN.

WE PASSED OUR OLD SCHOOL AND REACHED THE RAILWAY STATION. TRAIN CARS WAITED ON THE TRACKS. "MAX TEN HORSES" WAS MARKED ON THE SIDE OF THE CARS. EIGHTY JEWS WERE PUT INTO EACH WAGON.

OUR TRAIN STOPPED AT SEVERAL STATIONS. I WOULD STRETCH MY HEAD OUT THROUGH THE BARS. PEOPLE STARED. I CALLED OUT TO THEM, "PLEASE, *PLEASE*, COULD YOU GIVE US SOME WATER?" BUT THEY ONLY STOOD THERE. SOME PRETENDED NOT TO HEAR.

WE STARTED TO PRAY TO GOD THAT OUR JOURNEY WOULD END. IT WAS SO HIDEOUS IN THE TRAIN CAR THAT EVEN DEATH WOULD'VE BEEN BETTER.

WHEN WE JUMPED DOWN AT THE PLATFORM, I HEARD THE COMMANDS--"MEN, GATHER OVER THERE," AND, "WOMEN, OVER THERE."

EVERYTHING HAPPENED SO QUICKLY. WHEN I TURNED, THE GROUP OF MEN HAD ALREADY LEFT. I NEVER GOT TO HUG MY FATHER THAT ONE LAST TIME.

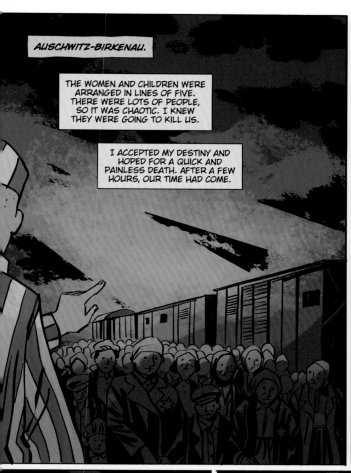

AUSCHWITZ-BIRKENAU.

THE WOMEN AND CHILDREN WERE ARRANGED IN LINES OF FIVE. THERE WERE LOTS OF PEOPLE, SO IT WAS CHAOTIC. I KNEW THEY WERE GOING TO KILL US.

I ACCEPTED MY DESTINY AND HOPED FOR A QUICK AND PAINLESS DEATH. AFTER A FEW HOURS, OUR TIME HAD COME.

THE S.S. OFFICER JUST STARED AT US. LATER WE LEARNED HE WAS THE NOTORIOUS DR. JOSEF MENGELE. HE LOOKED AT MUM AND POINTED TO THE LEFT. WE WERE SUPPOSED TO CONTINUE IN THE OTHER DIRECTION. THEY TOLD US TO UNDRESS. THE FACT THAT WE WERE UNDRESSING IN FRONT OF MEN DIDN'T EVEN SEEM TO MATTER.

WE TOOK OUR CLOTHES OFF AND PUT THEM IN A PILE, BUT KEPT OUR SHOES. I SQUEEZED MY BLACK BOOTS IN MY HANDS. WHEN I REALIZED WE WOULDN'T GET OUR CLOTHES BACK, I STUFFED MY LAST BELONGING, MY TOOTHBRUSH AND MY SILVER NECKLACE, INTO MY SHOES.

THEY TOOK AWAY THE LAST OF WHAT MADE US HUMAN. WE ALL LOOKED THE SAME. BUT WHERE WAS MY SISTER? I SHOUTED HER NAME DESPERATELY, UNTIL OUR EYES FINALLY MET. SHE TOOK MY HAND AND NEVER LET IT GO.

THEY PUSHED US INTO THE COLD WATER OF THE SHOWER ROOMS.

I WAS STILL ALIVE WHEN MORNING CAME. I WENT TO ONE OF THE POLISH JEWS WHO HAD ALREADY SPENT SOME TIME IN AUSCHWITZ.

"WHEN WILL OUR MUMS ARRIVE?" I ASKED. SHE STARED AT ME LIKE I WAS OUT OF MY MIND.

DO YOU SEE THAT CHIMNEY?

YES?

INSIDE, YOUR PARENTS WILL BURN. YOU'LL NEVER SEE THEM AGAIN.

THIS IS NOT A HOME. THIS IS AN EXTERMINATION CAMP.

ONE DAY, WE HEARD THAT TWO HUNDRED WOMEN WERE NEEDED FOR LABOR. WE ARRIVED IN HAMBURG AND WERE TRANSPORTED TO A CAMP. WE WOULD STAY THERE FOR THE COMING DAYS.

WE SWITCHED CAMPS MANY TIMES BEFORE WE ARRIVED IN HAMBURG-EIDELSTEDT.

AS LONG AS WE COULD WORK, WE GOT TO LIVE. IT WAS RAINY AND COLD AND THERE WAS LITTLE FOOD. EVERY NIGHT, AIR RAID ALARMS SOUNDED AND BOMBS FELL ALL AROUND US.

A YEAR PASSED AND I REALIZED, WITH TEARS IN MY EYES, THAT IT WAS MY BIRTHDAY.

WHEN WE GOT BACK FROM WORK THAT EVENING, MY FRIENDS STARTED TO WHISPER TO EACH OTHER.

AFTER A WHILE THEY CALLED FOR ME.

AND THERE ON ONE OF OUR BEDS, THEY HAD PREPARED SEVERAL PRESENTS.

HÉDI GAVE ME A PIECE OF BREAD. SOMEONE ELSE GAVE ME SOME TOILET PAPER AND JAM. ANOTHER ONE GAVE ME A SHOELACE. I STILL HAD MY BLACK BOOTS, BUT HADN'T HAD ANY LACES. FINALLY, I HAD LACES TOO.

I INSISTED ON DIVIDING THE BREAD BETWEEN ALL OF US. IT WAS A MARVELOUS BIRTHDAY.

IN THE SPRING OF 1945, WE KNEW THE GERMANS WERE LOSING THE WAR. THE QUESTION WAS WHETHER WE COULD LIVE TO SEE THE LIBERATION. THEN THE GERMANS CLOSED THE CAMP--WE WERE BEING SENT ELSEWHERE. WE HEARD A RUMOR THAT WE WERE TO BE KILLED. WE BOARDED ANOTHER TRAIN WITH NO IDEA WHERE WE WERE GOING.

THE TRAIN STOPPED IN THE MIDDLE OF THE NIGHT. LOUD NOISES AND GUNSHOTS CAME FROM THE WOODS. SCARED TO DEATH, WE WAITED IN THE TRAIN CAR, THINKING WE'D BE SHOT IF WE LEFT.

EVENTUALLY THE TRAIN CONTINUED.

KTHUMM

BOOM

BRAKKA

BRAKKA

BRAKKA

BERGEN-BELSEN.

THE PRISONERS THAT WE MET LOOKED MORE DEAD THAN ALIVE.

"IS THERE A GAS CHAMBER HERE?" WE ASKED. "NO," THEY ANSWERED. "THERE IS NO GAS CHAMBER-- NO WORK, AND NO FOOD."

WE WERE RELIEVED THAT THERE WERE NO GAS CHAMBERS, BUT IT ALSO FELT GOOD TO KNOW THERE WAS NO WORK.

WE GOT TO OUR BARRACK. NOTHING HAPPENED. WE JUST SAT OR LAID ON OUR BUNKS. NO ONE CARED ABOUT US.

THE DAYS PASSED, AND THERE WAS NO FOOD.

WE FOUND SOME WATER IN AN OLD TOILET. WE WOULDN'T HAVE SURVIVED IF WE HADN'T FOUND THAT.

ONE DAY A FRIEND CAME INTO OUR BARRACK.

I SAW FOREIGN SOLDIERS. I THINK THEY'RE ENGLISH.

FROM THE WINDOW, I COULD SEE SOLDIERS IN GREEN UNIFORMS. I WENT OUTSIDE TO SEE IF SHE WAS RIGHT.

BERGEN-BELSEN WAS LIBERATED BY BRITISH TROOPS.

DURING THE LIBERATION, WE DIDN'T CELEBRATE. WE COULDN'T. ALL WE COULD THINK ABOUT WAS FOOD. THE BRITISH WERE SHOCKED BY THE SIGHT OF US. THEY GAVE US CANS OF PEAS, PORK, AND BROWN BEANS.

WE TORE THE CANS OPEN AND POURED THE FOOD INTO OUR MOUTHS. EVERYONE THAT ATE GOT SICK, AND MANY DIED. WE HADN'T HAD ANY FOOD FOR SO LONG THAT SUDDENLY WE WERE EATING OURSELVES TO DEATH.

AFTER A WHILE, OUR SAVIORS REALIZED THEY HAD TO FIND ANOTHER WAY TO FEED US. THEY SET UP A HOSPITAL AND FED US SLOWLY. WE STARTED TO RECOVER.

ONE DAY A KNOCK CAME AT OUR DOOR. THREE WOMEN FROM THE SWEDISH RED CROSS ASKED US IF WE WANTED TO GO TO SWEDEN.

ALL THE SURVIVORS COULD SPEND SIX MONTHS RECOVERING IN SWEDEN. AFTER THAT WE WOULD BE SENT BACK TO OUR OWN COUNTRIES.

OUR COUSIN SUSSIE, HÉDI, AND I HAD PROMISED EACH OTHER WE'D STAY TOGETHER NO MATTER WHAT. WE ALL DECIDED THAT IT WAS THE RIGHT THING TO DO.

A SHIP TOOK US TO MALMOE, WHERE WE STOOD ON SWEDISH SOIL FOR THE FIRST TIME.

IN MALMOE, WE WERE HOSTED IN THE LINNÉ SCHOOL. DOCTORS EXAMINED US AND WE WERE GIVEN FOOD AND CLOTHES.

WE STAYED THERE FOR THREE WEEKS IN A KIND OF QUARANTINE. THEY WERE AFRAID WE WOULD SPREAD DISEASES TO THE LOCALS.

THE FIRST THING WE DID AT LINNÉ SCHOOL WAS EAT. WE ATE AND ATE. WHAT WE COULDN'T EAT, WE HID UNDER OUR PILLOWS. WHO KNEW IF WE'D EVER GET FOOD AGAIN?

WE ARRIVED IN AN OLD GUEST HOUSE OUTSIDE OF A TOWN CALLED ALINGSÅS. A BEAUTIFUL AND SMALL PLACE CALLED HJÄLMARED. THERE, REFUGEES WERE WELCOME.

NEXT STOP WAS A REFUGEE CAMP OUTSIDE OF STOCKHOLM, AT LOVÖ. THAT IS WHERE HÉDI'S LIFE AND MY OWN LIFE WERE SAVED.

IN STOCKHOLM I MET HANS FRÄNKEL. THE JEWISH COMMUNITY HAD ARRANGED A DANCE FOR THE YOUTH.

I WORE A RED DRESS. WHEN HANS LAID EYES ON ME, HE TOLD HIS FRIEND, "I'M GOING TO MARRY HER."

AND THAT'S WHAT HE DID.

Livia Fränkel lives in Stockholm. She has three children, six grandchildren, and five great grandchildren. For many years, Livia has worked for the Survivors of the Holocaust Association and is often in schools, telling her story. In 1992, Livia's sister Hédi published a book telling the story of their experiences during the war.

I WAS BORN IN FRANKFURT, GERMANY. MY DAD WAS A GOLDSMITH AND HE OWNED HIS OWN JEWELRY SHOP.

WE WERE LIVING IN LODZ WHEN THE GERMANS ATTACKED POLAND.

Selma

ONE YEAR AFTER THE CRYSTAL NIGHT, THE GERMANS CAME AND BURNED ALL OF THE SYNAGOGUES IN LODZ TO THE GROUND.

THEY TOLD US THAT ALL OF THE JEWS HAD TO BE GATHERED TOGETHER IN ONE PLACE.

WE SEARCHED FOR A PLACE TO STAY. THE GERMANS WENT FROM HOUSE TO HOUSE TO TRY AND SPEED UP THEIR SORTING PROCESS.

FOR EVERY FAMILY THAT HADN'T LEFT THEIR HOMES YET, THE GERMANS WOULD SHOOT EITHER THE FATHER OR THE ELDEST SON TO DEATH. THE REST OF THE FAMILY WOULD BE FORCED AWAY WHILE THE DEAD WERE LEFT LYING IN THE STREET.

MY BROTHER SAMUEL WAS SHOT BY GERMANS OUTSIDE HIS GIRLFRIEND'S HOUSE. HE HAD BROKEN THE CURFEW IN ORDER TO HELP HER AND HER MOM MOVE INTO THE GHETTO.

WE MOVED INTO THE GHETTO A FEW DAYS LATER.

WE HAD TO PAY FOR THE BARBED WIRE FENCES AND THE WALLS THAT SURROUNDED THE GHETTO. ON MAY 1, THE GERMANS SEALED THE GHETTO, AND WE COULDN'T LEAVE.

THERE WAS NO FOOD. WE WERE STARVING.

FIVE THOUSAND PEOPLE DIED FROM STARVATION DURING THE FIRST SIX MONTHS IN THE GHETTO.

MY SISTER ANNA WAS CAPTURED ON THE STREET.

WE SPENT A LONG TIME LOOKING FOR HER, BUT MUCH LATER, WE FOUND OUT WHAT HAD HAPPENED.

MY DAD WORKED IN THE WOOD INDUSTRY, SO I STARTED TO WORK ALONGSIDE HIM. WE TOOK THE WORKERS TO AND FROM THE FIELD. IT WAS A LONG TRIP.

ONE DAY AS I WAS LEAVING WORK, I COULDN'T FIND MY DAD. SOMEONE TOLD ME HE HAD FAINTED AND THAT MOM HAD TO DRAG HIM HOME ON A WAGON.

TWO WEEKS LATER, HE DIED FROM STARVATION.

DURING THE HIGH HOLIDAYS THE GERMANS ANNOUNCED A CURFEW. WE WERE SO DEVASTATED THAT WE COULDN'T EVEN GATHER IN THE LITTLE FREE TIME THAT WE HAD. A RUMOR SPREAD THAT ALL THE SICK PEOPLE, THE ELDERLY, AND THE CHILDREN WOULD BE SENT AWAY. ORPHANAGES, OLD FOLKS' HOMES, AND HOSPITALS WERE ALL CLEARED OUT. IT WAS HORRIFYING. I WAS SO SCARED.

MY MOM WAS TAKEN, BUT LUCKILY SHE ESCAPED. SHE HID IN A CELLAR ALL NIGHT AND SNUCK BACK TO US IN THE MORNING.

BY AUGUST, ONLY A FRACTION OF THE THREE HUNDRED AND FIFTY THOUSAND PEOPLE IN THE GHETTO WAS LEFT. THE OFFICERS TOLD US THAT WE'D BE MOVED SOMEWHERE ELSE. MY MOM, MY SISTER PAULA, AND I WENT TO THE STATION.

WE CARRIED OUR THINGS IN RUCKSACKS. THE NEXT MORNING, WE WERE LOADED ONTO A TRAIN, AND TRAVELED ALL DAY. THE RAILWAY TRACK HAD BEEN DAMAGED BY BOMBS. AT NIGHT THE TRAIN STOOD STILL BY THE SIDE OF THE TRACKS.

IN THE MORNING WE ARRIVED AT A RAILWAY YARD, IN A CHAOS OF COMMANDER'S ROARS, WHISTLES, AND OUR OWN SCREAMS. PRISONERS IN STRIPED CLOTHES SEPARATED THE MEN FROM THE WOMEN.

THEY BROUGHT US TO THE CAPTAIN OF THE CAMP. HE POINTED TO THE RIGHT OR THE LEFT WITH HIS LEATHER WHIP. PLAYFULLY AND CALMLY, HE DECIDED WHO LIVED AND WHO DIED.

HE CHOSE MY MOM AND KILLED HER ALONG WITH THOUSANDS OF WOMEN AND CHILDREN THAT DAY.

AFTER THE FIRST NIGHT WE WERE COMMANDED TO MARCH NAKED IN THE COURTYARD. THE CHOSEN ONES WOULD BE PUT TO WORK.

WE HAD TO RUN IN FRONT OF THE S.S. MEN, NAKED. MY SISTER AND I WERE AMONG THE FIVE HUNDRED AND TWENTY SELECTED FOR SLAVE LABOR AT KRUPPS WEAPON FACTORY IN BERLIN.

WE WERE TAKEN BACK TO THE RAILWAY. WE LAY ON THE GROUND IN THE DRIZZLING RAIN, WAITING FOR THE TRAINS TO TAKE US TO BERLIN IN THE MORNING.

IN THE MIDDLE OF THE NIGHT A WOMAN CAME TO ME AND PAULA. SHE SAID THAT SHE HAD BEEN WITH OUR SISTER ANNA WHEN SHE WAS CAPTURED IN THE GHETTO.

ANNA WAS NOT ALIVE.

DURING THE FIRST TWO WEEKS IN BERLIN, WE WERE KEPT IN QUARANTINE. AFTER THAT WE STARTED WORKING AT KRUPPS. MY SLAVE NUMBER WAS ONE HUNDRED AND FOURTEEN. PAULA'S WAS ONE HUNDRED AND FIFTEEN.

ONE SUNDAY IN FEBRUARY 1945, ALL OF BERLIN CAUGHT FIRE. THE WARM AND SUNNY DAY TURNED INTO NIGHT BECAUSE OF ALL THE SMOKE. WE SAT IN THE TRENCHES WITHOUT A ROOF.

THE BOMBS FELL ALL AROUND US. ONE OF THE BARRACKS BURNED DOWN. WE REALIZED THAT THE END WAS CLOSE.

THE RUSSIANS WERE CLOSING IN ON BERLIN.

WE WERE EVACUATED TO ORANIENBURG.

TWO DAYS LATER, WE WERE MOVED TO A WOMEN'S CAMP IN RAVENSBRÜCK.

IT ONLY TOOK US SIX HOURS TO GET THERE.

I FELL APART WHEN I SAW THE RED CROSS BUSES.

SCHWEDEN

WE STAYED OVERNIGHT IN DENMARK. WHEN WE ARRIVED IN SWEDEN, I STILL CLUTCHED MY RED CROSS PACKAGE.

IN LUND, THE DOCTOR NOTED IN MY CHART--TUBERCULOSIS, WEIGHT SIXTY-ONE POUNDS.

HITLER HAD STOLEN ANOTHER THREE YEARS FROM ME. I HAD TO BE CUT OFF FROM THE WORLD WHILE I RECOVERED.

PAULA AND I DREAMT OF GOING TO PALESTINE, BUT WE COULDN'T GO UNTIL I WAS WELL ENOUGH.

I FINALLY LEFT THE SANATORIUM, AND LATER MARRIED ERIK BENGTSSON.

IN JANUARY 1949, PAULA LEFT FOR ISRAEL.*

E STATE OF ISRAEL WAS ANNOUNCED IN 1948

FROM OUR LARGE FAMILY, PAULA AND I WERE THE ONLY TWO SURVIVORS.

After leaving the sanatorium outside Varberg,
Selma Bengtsson stayed in Varberg for the rest of
her life. Together with her husband Erik, Selma had a son
and many grandchildren. Selma and her family remained
close to her sister Paula and her family in Israel.

MAKÓ, SOUTHEASTERN HUNGARY.

Susanna

MY MUM AND DAD RAN A SMALL GROCERY STORE. WE SPENT ALMOST ALL OUR TIME IN THE STORE AND THE LITTLE KITCHEN.

MY FAMILY WAS POOR. WE LIVED ON WHAT LITTLE WE HAD. WE DIDN'T HAVE A RADIO OR A TELEPHONE.

ALL OF THE NEWSPAPERS IN HUNGARY WERE CENSORED THEN. YOU HAD TO READ BETWEEN THE LINES AND TRY TO GUESS WHAT WAS ACTUALLY GOING ON IN EUROPE.

WE HAD A TEACHER THAT HATED US BECAUSE WE WERE JEWISH. SHE MADE US WRITE OUR ESSAYS ON SATURDAYS. TO ME THAT WASN'T A PROBLEM-- MY FAMILY WASN'T RELIGIOUS AND WE DIDN'T CELEBRATE SHABBAT OR ANY OTHER JEWISH HOLIDAYS.

THROUGHOUT THE SPRING SEMESTER, THE TEACHER EXPLAINED WHERE THE GERMANS WERE. SHE ADDED, "THEY'LL BE HERE SOON AND WE'LL GET RID OF ALL THE JEWS." SHE REPEATED THAT TO US EVERY LESSON.

WE HEARD THAT ALL JEWS IN MAKÓ HAD BEEN ORDERED TO MOVE TO TWO DIFFERENT, WORN-DOWN GHETTOS IN THE TOWN.

MY DAD WANTED US TO RENT A ROOM AT THE OLD FOLKS' HOME. THERE WAS ONE AVAILABLE THERE AND IT WOULD BE CHEAPER FOR US.

MY DAD, MUM, AND I WERE INVITED TO CELEBRATE PASSOVER AT THE DIRECTOR'S HOME. THAT MEANT A LOT TO ME. AT HOME, WE NEVER CELEBRATED THE JEWISH HOLIDAYS.

THE DIRECTOR AND HIS FAMILY HAD ARRIVED IN HUNGARY FROM ROMANIA. BUT ONE DAY, THEY WERE JUST GONE.

WE FOUND OUT THAT ALL JEWS WITHOUT HUNGARIAN CITIZENSHIP WERE TO BE DEPORTED. THEN MILITARY POLICE BANGED ON OUR DOOR AND YELLED THAT WE HAD TO PACK UP AND BRING ENOUGH FOOD FOR A THREE-DAY TRIP.

MY MUM IMMEDIATELY STARTED BOILING EGGS. EGGS WERE EASY TO KEEP GOOD IN THE SUMMER HEAT. WE PACKED SOME BED LINEN, CLOTHES, AND COOKING UTENSILS.

WE WERE TAKEN ON TRUCKS TO SZEGED, THE SECOND LARGEST TOWN IN HUNGARY. THEY PUT US IN A TENT CAMP IN THE OUTSKIRTS OF THE CITY.

SINCE WE WERE AFRAID OF BEING ROBBED AT NIGHT, WE BROUGHT EVERYTHING WE HAD INTO OUR TENT, AND WE SLEPT OUTSIDE, ON THE GROUND.

THEY FORCED US TO LEAVE ALL OUR VALUABLE THINGS BEHIND. JEWELRY AND MONEY, EVEN PENS. THEY THREATENED THAT THEY'D SHOOT EVERY TENTH ONE OF US IF WE DIDN'T OBEY.

I LATER FOUND OUT THAT MY DAD, IN SPITE OF THE RULES, KEPT A LITTLE PENCIL. THANKS TO THAT PENCIL HE WROTE A DIARY IN HIS CALENDAR THAT HE KEPT THE WHOLE TIME HE WAS IN THE CAMP.

AFTER A FEW DAYS, WE WERE TAKEN TO A BRICKYARD IN SZEGED. THERE MUST HAVE BEEN TWO THOUSAND JEWS, ALL FROM MY HOMETOWN. WE MADE BEDS FROM STRAW AND SLEPT CLOSE BESIDE EACH OTHER.

WE WERE DIVIDED INTO THREE GROUPS AT THE BRICKYARD. MY FAMILY WAS IN GROUP TWO.

MY GREAT AUNT HANNA WAS THERE TOO, BUT SHE DISAPPEARED. I NEVER SAW HER AGAIN.

I REMEMBER HOW IT FELT, BEING STOWED INTO THE TRAIN CARS.

THE TRAIN WAS VERY LONG.

IT STOPPED SEVERAL TIMES AT MANY DIFFERENT STATIONS. IT JUST STOOD THERE, STILL.

THROUGH THE SMALL OPENINGS IN THE TRAIN CAR, WE TRIED TO KEEP TRACK OF WHERE WE WERE GOING. ONE OF US SAW THE NAMES OF STATIONS THAT WE PASSED AND KNEW THAT WE WERE HEADING NORTH.

WE ARRIVED IN KOŠICE BY THE BORDER TOWARD SLOVAKIA, AND THE TRAIN STOPPED.

NAZI TYSKLAND

SLOVAKIEN

KOŠICE

WE LATER FOUND OUT THE RAILWAY HAD BEEN BOMBED, AND THAT WAS WHY WE COULDN'T KEEP GOING.

UNGERN

WE PASSED THROUGH BUDAPEST AND CONTINUED INTO AUSTRIA. FINALLY, WE ARRIVED IN STRASSHOF.

IT WAS DARK WHEN WE GOT THERE. PEOPLE EVERYWHERE. MANY LOST SIGHT OF EACH OTHER IN THE CROWD. THROUGH THE NIGHT YOU COULD HEAR PEOPLE SHOUTING EACH OTHER'S NAMES, LOOKING FOR FRIENDS AND FAMILY.

WE WERE DISINFECTED, ALONG WITH OUR LUGGAGE. MEN AND WOMEN WERE SEPARATED.

IT WAS EMBARRASSING FOR THE WOMEN. THE SOLDIERS WATCHED THEM CLOSELY. IT WAS NOT COMMON FOR A WOMAN TO BE NAKED WITH A MAN, NOT EVEN WITH HER HUSBAND.

AFTER THEY SHOWERED US, THEY FORCED US INTO THE BARRACKS. ONE WEEK LATER WE WERE PUT ON A TRAIN AGAIN, TO BRUCK AN DER LEITHA IN AUSTRIA.

WE FOUND OURSELVES IN SOME KIND OF BOARDING HOUSE AND THE ADULTS WERE PUT TO WORK IN THE GARDEN.

A MAN APPEARED WITH A HORSE AND A WAGON. HE BROUGHT US TO A FARM WHERE WE WOULD WORK. WE STAYED IN A BARN THAT WAS DIVIDED INTO TWO ROOMS.

WE SLEPT WITH TEN TO TWELVE PEOPLE IN EACH ROOM. OUR BEDS WERE MADE OF STRAW AND SET UP ON THE FLOOR.

THE YOUNG ONES DIDN'T HAVE TO WORK. NOT IN THE BEGINNING. MY DAD HAD A BAD LEG, SO HE DIDN'T HAVE TO WORK EITHER. INSTEAD, THE OTHER CHILDREN AND I HELPED IN THE KITCHEN. THE HOUSE-WIFE WAS MARRIED TO THE MAN WHO PICKED US UP.

HE WAS THE SUPERVISOR OF THE FIELDS AND HE WAS NICE TO US.

THE HOUSE-WIFE WASN'T NICE LIKE HIM. SHE WAS MEAN. WE WERE ALL AFRAID OF HER.

SHE WOULD LET US HELP, BUT SHE WATCHED US CLOSELY WITH MEAN EYES.

WE WERE SERVED POTATOES AND BEANS TWICE A DAY WITH BREAD.

ON SUNDAYS, WE ATE MEAT. THE CHILDREN WERE GIVEN MILK EVERY DAY. LIFE AT THE FARM WAS ALL RIGHT. WE WANTED TO STAY THERE UNTIL THE WAR ENDED.

ONE DAY, GERMAN SOLDIERS ARRIVED WITH A GROUP OF POLISH WOMEN. THE WOMEN STAYED IN ANOTHER PART OF THE FARM.

THE GERMANS FINALLY FORCED ALL OF US TO THE FIELDS. IT WAS HEAVY WORK. AN OLD WOMAN DIED THERE.

AT THE END OF NOVEMBER, THEY TOLD US TO PACK OUR THINGS.

THEY TOOK US BACK TO STRASSHOF. WE SPENT THE FIRST NIGHT OUTSIDE.

WE STAYED IN STRASSHOF FOR ABOUT A WEEK UNTIL THEY PUT US ON ANOTHER TRAIN.

THREE DAYS LATER, THE TRAIN STOPPED. WE DRAGGED OUR THINGS A VERY LONG WAY TOWARD SOME BARRACKS.

THE CAMP WAS SURROUNDED BY BARBED WIRE AND DIVIDED INTO DIFFERENT SECTIONS.

NONE OF US HAD EVER HEARD OF BERGEN-BELSEN UNTIL WE FOUND OURSELVES THERE.

MY FAMILY AND AROUND TWO THOUSAND OTHER PEOPLE CAME FROM SZEGED. WE WERE PLACED IN THE SAME GROUP.

OUR FAMILY OF THREE WAS ASSIGNED TWO BUNKS. SINCE MY DAD COULDN'T CLIMB, HE GOT HIS OWN BUNK AT THE BOTTOM.

FOR BREAKFAST THEY FED US SOME KIND OF STRANGE DRINK. A MIX BETWEEN SOUP AND STEW.

EVERY THIRD DAY WE HAD A THIN PIECE OF BREAD. IT WAS HEAVY AS CLAY.

MY MUM MADE SURE THAT WE SAVED THE BREAD FOR THE DAYS WHEN WE WOULDN'T HAVE IT. WE STILL STARVED. AND IT WAS HORRIBLE.

THE SECTIONS IN THE CAMP WERE DIVIDED BY A THICK WALL. WE USED TO STAND BY THE GATES AND LOOK OUT.

EVERY DAY WE SAW CARRIAGES LOADED WITH NAKED CORPSES. THE BODIES LOOKED LIKE SKELETONS.

THERE WERE ONLY FAMILIES IN OUR CAMP. IN SOME SECTIONS, WOMEN WERE KEPT SEPARATE FROM MEN.

GERMAN SOLDIERS WATCHED OVER THE CAMP FROM THEIR GUARD TOWER.

FROM THE TOWER THEY CONSTANTLY SHINED THEIR SEARCHLIGHT ON US.

THE SEARCHLIGHT FOLLOWED US BACK AND FORTH AT NIGHT WHEN WE USED THE TOILET.

THE DRY TOILET WAS A LARGE ROOM WITH A BENCH WHERE YOU SAT DOWN AND DID WHAT YOU HAD TO DO.

BOTH MEN AND WOMEN USED THE SAME TOILET. LIFE WAS HORRIFYING IN BERGEN-BELSEN.

WE PRAYED AND BEGGED GOD THAT A BOMB WOULD JUST END IT ALL.

THAT'S HOW BAD THINGS WERE. WE BEGGED FOR DEATH. WE SAW NO LIGHT.

ALL OF A SUDDEN IN THE BEGINNING OF APRIL 1945, WE LEFT BERGEN-BELSEN.

WE HAD BEEN IN THE CAMP SINCE EARLY DECEMBER. WE WERE STARVING AND WEAK.

THOSE WHO COULD LEFT BY FOOT. BUT MY DAD WAS TOO WEAK TO WALK. ME AND MY MUM DIDN'T WANT TO LEAVE HIM.

WE WATCHED EVERYONE GO ONE BY ONE.

TRUCKS CAME TO TAKE THE ONES STILL LEFT BEHIND. WE STRUGGLED, FRANTICALLY TRYING TO CATCH UP WITH EVERYONE.

WE COULDN'T REACH THE OTHERS BECAUSE MY DAD WAS SO WEAK. OUR FAMILY FINALLY MADE IT ONTO THE LAST TRUCK THAT LEFT THE CAMP.

WE WERE TAKEN TO THE STATION WHERE A TRAIN STOOD WAITING.

THE TRAIN WAS ALREADY FULL WHEN WE ARRIVED. IT WAS SUCH A DISAPPOINTMENT. THE TRAIN WAS SUPPOSED TO BE OUR SAVIOR.

SUDDENLY, A WOMAN SHOUTED.

WE HAVE ROOM FOR THE CHILD!

BUT MY DAD DIDN'T WANT ME TO GO.

BRING OUR CHILD *BACK!* IF WE'RE GOING TO DIE, THEN WE SHOULD DIE *TOGETHER!*

MY MUM GRABBED ME. THE TRAIN LEFT THE STATION. HAD I BEEN ON THE TRAIN, I WOULD'VE BEEN SEPARATED FROM MY PARENTS.

THERE WERE ABOUT FORTY PEOPLE LEFT ON THE PLATFORM. ONE TRAIN STOOD ON THE TRACKS, EMPTY. WE CLIMBED INTO THE TRAIN CAR.

THOSE THAT DIDN'T HAVE THE STRENGTH TO CLIMB STAYED ON THE GROUND. ONE OF THEM DIED DURING THE NIGHT.

NO ONE KNEW WHAT WAS GOING TO HAPPEN. WE COULDN'T DO ANYTHING BUT WAIT.

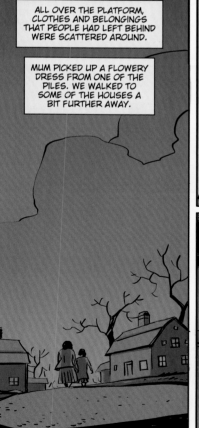

ALL OVER THE PLATFORM, CLOTHES AND BELONGINGS THAT PEOPLE HAD LEFT BEHIND WERE SCATTERED AROUND.

MUM PICKED UP A FLOWERY DRESS FROM ONE OF THE PILES. WE WALKED TO SOME OF THE HOUSES A BIT FURTHER AWAY.

IN FRONT OF A LARGE VILLA, MUM WAVED THE DRESS AT A WOMAN, WHO OPENED HER DOOR.

THE LADY WENT BACK INTO HER HOUSE AND CAME OUT WITH TWO PIECES OF BREAD. SHE DIDN'T EVEN TAKE THE DRESS.

MUM AND I WENT BACK AND SHARED THE BREAD WITH MY DAD.

CHFF
CHFF
CHFF

A TRAIN IS COMING!

PSCCHHHH

OUT! OUT! HURRY UP!

THE WEAKEST OF US GOT HELP FROM OTHER PRISONERS. MANY OF THE DEAD WERE CARRIED.

THE MEN WERE THIN AS SKELETONS. SUDDENLY, THE PLATFORM WAS COMPLETELY CROWDED. I FOUND A SWEDISH TURNIP, BUT ONE OF THE MEN HAD ALSO LAID EYES ON IT.

GIVE US FOOD! PLEASE!

A GERMAN SOLDIER STARTED TO BEAT THE MAN. HE HIT HIM AND HIT HIM UNTIL THE MAN LAY ON THE GROUND, DEAD.

ALL MEN WERE TAKEN TO THE CAMP, BUT MANY DEAD BODIES WERE LEFT LYING THERE ON THE PLATFORM.

FINALLY, WE WERE TAKEN BACK TO BERGEN-BELSEN, THIS TIME TO A DIFFERENT SECTION. THIS WAS A CAMP FOR DUTCH JEWS.*

ONLY ABOUT TEN PEOPLE WERE LEFT IN THAT CAMP. THEY HAD TYPHUS, WHICH WAS VERY CONTAGIOUS.

THEY ALL LAID ON THEIR BUNKS.

AS LONG AS MY MUM COULD STAND UPRIGHT, SHE WENT AROUND HELPING PEOPLE AND GIVING THEM WATER.

TOWARD THE END, JUST BEFORE THE LIBERATION, MY MUM WAS ALSO WEAK AND ILL.

* SUSANNA LATER LEARNED THAT SHE WAS IN BERGEN-BELSEN AT THE SAME TIME THAT ANNE FRANK WAS. BERGEN-BELSEN WAS THE CAMP WHERE ANNE FRANK DIED.

ON APRIL 15, BERGEN-BELSEN WAS LIBERATED.

TWO DAYS LATER MY DAD DIED.

HE LEFT SOME THINGS IN A PAPER BAG THAT HE HAD KEPT FROM HOME.

IN THE BAG WERE HIS GLASSES, A PENCIL, AND HIS DIARY.

LATER I STARTED WRITING WHERE HE HAD STOPPED.

MY MUM DIED A LITTLE OVER A WEEK AFTER DAD DID. SHE COULD HARDLY LIFT HER HEAD. A FEW DAYS LATER EVEN I WAS BOUND TO MY BUNK.

NAKED AND SWADDLED IN BLANKETS, WE WERE CARRIED OUT OF THE BARRACKS AND INTO MILITARY AMBULANCES.

BUT THROUGH IT ALL I KEPT THE BAG WITH THE THINGS MY DAD HAD LEFT BEHIND.

WE WERE DELOUSED AND BATHED.

WHAT A DIRTY CHILD!

I HAD STUDIED GERMAN IN JEWISH SCHOOL. I EXPLAINED TO HER THAT I WASN'T ABLE TO CLEAN MYSELF OR CHANGE MY CLOTHES FOR FIVE MONTHS, BECAUSE WE DIDN'T HAVE ANY WATER.

SHE DIDN'T ANSWER.

WE HAD NO CLOTHES SO EVERYONE WALKED AROUND SWADDLED IN BLANKETS. IT LOOKED LIKE A GHOST TOWN.

EVEN AFTER THE LIBERATION, MANY PEOPLE DIED.

WE GOT SOME CLOTHES TO WEAR AND SOME SOAP AND TOOTHBRUSHES. SINCE I WAS THE ONLY CHILD, I GOT AN EXTRA TRUNK THAT HAD ROOM FOR A CHECKERED WINTER COAT.

WHEN WE FINALLY ARRIVED IN SWEDEN, WE COULD HOLD EVERYTHING WE OWNED IN THREE SMALL TRUNKS.

MY DAD'S JOURNAL IS KEPT
IN THE BERGEN-BELSEN
ARCHIVES. THEY ALSO HAVE
HIS GLASSES AT THE MUSEUM.

Susanna Christensen was one of the first survivors to travel around to schools telling the story of her experiences during the Holocaust. Wherever she goes, everyone listens carefully, and she's met with great appreciation. She believes it's important for young people today to meet those who experienced the war—especially today, when she feels that the hatred of Jews is increasing again. She is not afraid for her own sake anymore, but hopes that her descendants never have to experience any of the things that she did.

Emerich

I HAVE EXPERIENCED THE UTMOST CONSEQUENCES OF HATRED AND VIOLENCE.

I'VE BEEN A PRISONER IN FIVE CONCENTRATION CAMPS. NOT A SINGLE HUMAN BEING SHOULD HAVE TO GO THROUGH OR SEE THE THINGS THAT I HAVE EXPERIENCED.

I WAS BORN IN WHAT WAS THEN CZECHOSLOVAKIA. TODAY IT'S CALLED VINOGRADOV, AND IT'S A PART OF UKRAINE.

I HAD A BIG FAMILY. MUM AND DAD, FOUR YOUNGER SISTERS, A GRANDMOTHER, SIX UNCLES, AND TWENTY-FOUR COUSINS.

AFTER OUR PART OF THE COUNTRY BECAME PART OF HUNGARY, OUR LIVES BECAME MUCH HARDER. THE ANTISEMITISM IN HUNGARY HAD BEEN A PART OF THE COUNTRY'S HISTORY FOR HUNDREDS OF YEARS. SUDDENLY, IT WAS A PART OF OUR LIVES TOO.

WE HOPED THAT THIS BAD DREAM WOULD END. BUT THINGS WOULD GET WORSE. MUCH WORSE.

AUSCHWITZ-BIRKENAU.

WE SAW GERMAN SOLDIERS AND OFFICERS. THEY KEPT THEIR DOGS READY TO JUMP ON US AT ANY MOMENT.

THEY MADE US FORM TWO LINES, ONE FOR MEN AND ONE FOR WOMEN AND CHILDREN. THEY TOLD US TO MOVE FORWARD SLOWLY.

AHEAD OF US, AN ELEGANT MAN STOOD ON A KIND OF STAGE. HE WAS AN OFFICER. HE DIDN'T SAY A WORD. HE JUST POINTED TO THE RIGHT OR LEFT. AS WE CAME CLOSER WE SAW HIS BLUE, ICE COLD EYES, STARING AT US.

LATER WE FOUND OUT THAT THE MAN DECIDING WHO LIVED AND WHO DIED WAS DR. JOSEF MENGELE. ELDERLY PEOPLE, PREGNANT WOMEN, CHILDREN, AND SICK PEOPLE, TO THE LEFT.

THOSE IN GOOD CONDITION, TO THE RIGHT. MY DAD HAD BEEN WOUNDED IN THE FIRST WORLD WAR, SO HE HAD A LIMP. I SQUEEZED HIS ARM HARD AND TRIED TO HOLD HIM UP SO THEY WOULDN'T NOTICE. WE GOT AWAY WITH IT AND ENDED UP ON THE RIGHT SIDE TOGETHER. MY MOTHER AND SIBLINGS WERE IN THE OTHER LINE.

MUM AND MY YOUNGEST SISTERS, MAGDALENA AND JUDITH, WERE SELECTED TO LIVE.

FROM THEN ON, I WAS CALLED ONLY BY MY NUMBER. THE OFFICERS TOLD US TO SIT DOWN AND WAIT.

WE COULD SEE A HIGH CHIMNEY.

AFTER AROUND FOUR WEEKS WE MOVED TO A SMALLER WORKING CAMP. OUR JOB WAS TO BREAK ROCKS.

MY DAD AND I USED SLEDGEHAMMERS. WE CARRIED THE SPLIT STONES WITH OUR BARE HANDS TO THE CARRIAGES.

THE STONES WERE USED FOR ROAD CONSTRUCTION. IT WAS HEAVY WORK AND ACCIDENTS HAPPENED ALL THE TIME.

WE HAD SO LITTLE FOOD, MANY DIED OF STARVATION. THEY USED HUNGER TO CONTROL THE PRISONERS.

WE WERE TIRED, WEAK, AND HAD NOTHING LEFT IN US TO RESIST.

OUR CAMP COMMANDER'S NAME WAS WULF.

HE'D CALL US SWINE AND DOGS, AND HIT US WITH HIS WOODEN CLUB.

HE SHOWERED US WITH HATRED. SOMETIMES, HE'D PUT SOMEONE OUTSIDE ALL NIGHT AND MAKE THEM STAND IN A BARREL FULL OF ICE-COLD WATER.

ALL THE WHILE, HE'D LOVE AND ADORE HIS GERMAN SHEPHERD.

TWO MONTHS BEFORE THE WAR ENDED THE GERMANS STILL BELIEVED THEY WERE WINNING. RATHER THAN LEAVING US IN THE CAMP, THEY FORCED US TO FLEE WITH THEM.

THERE WAS A RUMOR THAT ANYONE LEFT BEHIND WOULD EITHER BE TAKEN TO ANOTHER CAMP OR SHOT.

MY DAD WAS SUPPOSED TO BE LEFT BEHIND, BUT I TOOK HIM BY THE HAND AND DRAGGED HIM OUT...

NOBODY NOTICED. "AS LONG AS I LIVE," I TOLD HIM, "WE'LL BE TOGETHER." DAD GOT WEAKER AND WEAKER.

I HELD HIM CLOSE UNDER HIS ARM AS WE KEPT MARCHING WITH THE CROWD.

A SOLDIER APPROACHED US AND SAID THAT A HORSE AND CARRIAGE WAS IN THE BACK TO HOLD THE WEAK PEOPLE.

MY DAD WAS SO EXHAUSTED HE IMMEDIATELY SAID YES.

THAT WAS THE LAST TIME I SAW HIM.

LATER I FOUND OUT THAT WE WERE AMONG ABOUT THIRTY THOUSAND PRISONERS MARCHING. IN HISTORY BOOKS IT'S OFTEN CALLED THE MARCH OF DEATH. THERE WERE ONLY A FEW THOUSAND SURVIVORS OUT OF ALL OF US PRISONERS.

WE GOT TO A TRAIN STATION WHERE THERE WERE CARRIAGES AND WAGONS.

WE HAD TO LEAN ON EACH OTHER IN ORDER TO STAND UPRIGHT.

SUDDENLY, SOME GERMAN SOLDIERS STARTED THROWING BREAD AT US. MANY DIED IN THE CHAOS.

WE ARRIVED IN BUCHENWALD, A NOTORIOUS CONCENTRATION CAMP WHERE EVERYONE WAS WAITING FOR THE END TO COME.

THE GERMANS' ESCAPE CONTINUED. AFTER BUCHENWALD, THEY TOOK US TO THERESIENSTADT.

WHEN WE ARRIVED, THE GERMAN SOLDIERS HAD ALREADY LEFT.

ABOUT THREE WEEKS LATER, RUSSIAN FORCES LIBERATED THE PRISONERS.

A TYPHUS EPIDEMIC HAD BROKEN OUT IN THE CAMP AND MANY DIED.

I KNEW HOW TO SPEAK RUSSIAN, SO I ASKED THE TROOPS TO BRING ME WITH THEM.

I ENDED UP IN THE HOSPITAL.

Больница

A DOCTOR CARRIED ME TO THE BATHROOM. ON THE WAY THERE WE PASSED A MIRROR.

I SAW A SKELETON WITH LIVING EYES. I WAS TWENTY-ONE YEARS OLD, FIVE FEET AND SEVEN INCHES TALL, AND WEIGHED SEVENTY-FIVE POUNDS.

81

I WANTED TO GO HOME AS SOON AS POSSIBLE. A SMALL PART OF ME HOPED TO FIND SOMEONE FROM MY FAMILY WAITING THERE.

FINALLY, I GOT BACK TO MY HOMETOWN.

I'D DREAMT OF THAT MOMENT FOR SO LONG, DREAMT OF HOW IT WOULD FEEL TO BE FREE. I'D LONGED FOR AND IMAGINED HOW I WOULD GET BACK HOME.

I RAN AS FAST AS I COULD AND SEARCHED FOR OUR HOUSE. THERE IT WAS, SEALED WITH WOODEN PLANKS OVER THE WINDOWS AND THE DOOR. I PULLED THE BOARDS AWAY AND LOOKED INSIDE.

IT WAS COMPLETELY EMPTY. ALL OF OUR BELONGINGS, OUR FURNITURE, EVERYTHING WAS GONE.

I JUST HAD ONE THOUGHT IN MY HEAD--I NEED TO GET AWAY FROM HERE!

I RAN BACK TO THE STATION AND JUMPED ON A TRAIN THAT WAS ALREADY MOVING.

I DIDN'T CARE WHERE
THE TRAIN WAS GOING.
I TRAVELED FOR WEEKS
THROUGH A BROKEN EUROPE.

I PASSED THROUGH HUNGARY AND
AUSTRIA UNTIL I REACHED A LITTLE
TOWN IN THE SOUTH OF ITALY. I
FOUND A GROUP OF JEWISH KIDS
WHO HAD LIVED THROUGH SIMILAR
HORRORS AS ME.

WE DECIDED TO GO TO
PALESTINE. A FEW DAYS
BEFORE WE LEFT, I GOT SICK.
I'D CAUGHT TUBERCULOSIS
AND ENDED UP IN HOSPITAL.

THE SPARK OF LIFE IN ME
HAD DISAPPEARED. NOTHING
MATTERED. THEN SOMETHING
HAPPENED THAT CHANGED
EVERYTHING.

A FRIEND FROM THE GROUP CAME
RUNNING INTO THE HOSPITAL WITH
A PIECE OF PAPER IN HIS HAND.

THE LETTER WAS FROM MY COUSIN
WHO'D MOVED TO PALESTINE
BEFORE THE WAR. HE WROTE TO
TELL ME THAT ONE OF MY SISTERS
WAS ALIVE IN SWEDEN. IT WAS
SUCH AN EMOTIONAL EXPERIENCE,
SO SHOCKING AND BEAUTIFUL. I
GOT THAT SPARK OF LIFE BACK.

SOON MY SISTER CAME TO
SEE ME IN ITALY. SHE'D
BEEN WITH OUR SISTER
EDITH IN THE CAMP.

BUT EDITH HAD GOTTEN SICK
AND DIED A FEW WEEKS
BEFORE THE LIBERATION.

THE NAZIS COULD NEVER TAKE
THE LOVE THAT I'D EXPERIENCED
AS A CHILD AWAY FROM ME.

Emerich Roth arrived in Sweden in 1950, first and foremost to be with his sister Elisabeth. He studied and became a social worker and therapist. He has worked at prisons and as operating chief at a rehabilitation center for abused youth. He wanted to use his experience to help others. Emerich believes that knowledge of the Holocaust can teach us about the future. A generation without historical education will be defenseless in preventing history repeating itself.

Elisabeth

MY MOM DIDN'T HAVE MUCH FREE TIME. SHE WAS FULLY PREOCCUPIED WITH ME AND MY FOUR SIBLINGS AND TAKING CARE OF OUR HOME.

SOMETIMES I WOULD TRAVEL TO MY DAD'S COUSIN ILONA'S HOME. I HELPED HER TAKE CARE OF HER LITTLE BOY TOMIK. I LOVED HIM SO MUCH.

WE LIVED IN TERRACED HOUSES WITH MOSTLY JEWISH NEIGHBORS. WE WOULD LISTEN TO OUR NEIGHBORS' RADIOS IN THE COURTYARD.

THAT'S HOW WE HEARD THE NEWS. I REMEMBER SENSING THAT SOMETHING WAS VERY WRONG.

THEY ANNOUNCED THAT ALL JEWS HAD TO LEAVE THEIR HOMES AND MOVE TO ANOTHER STREET WHERE MOST JEWS ALREADY LIVED.

WE DIDN'T KNOW YET THAT THE SAME THING HAD BEEN HAPPENING IN CITIES ALL OVER OUR COUNTRY. WE MOVED TO THE GHETTO IN 1944.

I REMEMBER WALKING THROUGH TOWN, AND OUR NEIGHBORS STANDING BY THE SIDE OF THE ROAD, JUST WATCHING US.

COMPLETELY SILENT.

THERE WERE SO MANY OF US WHEN WE GOT TO AUSCHWITZ.

I DIDN'T THINK. I JUST FOLLOWED EVERYONE ELSE.

THEY TOLD US TO THROW OUR BAGS INTO A PILE.

MANY RAN TO THE PILE TO PICK SOMETHING OUT, SOME SMALL MEMORY.

THEY WERE IMMEDIATELY BEATEN. IT COST SOME OF THEM THEIR LIVES. I SNUCK MY BRACELET INTO MY SHOE.

BUT THEY TOOK MY SHOES TOO.

THEY SHOWERED US AND SHAVED OUR HAIR. THAT WAS THE LAST TIME I SAW MY MOM AND MY YOUNGER SISTERS, MAGDALENA AND JUDITH.

MY MOM WAS FORTY-ONE. MY SISTERS WERE TWELVE AND FOURTEEN YEARS OLD. I WAS SIXTEEN.

MY SISTER EDITH AND I WERE TOGETHER IN AUSCHWITZ FOR SIX MONTHS. THEN SHE GOT SICK.

I LEFT HER BEHIND. THAT STILL TORMENTS ME TODAY, BUT I KNEW THAT IF I DIDN'T LEAVE, I WOULD DIE TOO.

I CELEBRATED MY SEVENTEENTH BIRTHDAY IN AUSCHWITZ WITH MY FRIENDS.

MY DAD AND MY BROTHER WERE ALSO IN THE CAMP, BUT I DIDN'T KNOW IT AT THE TIME.

I MET MY DAD'S COUSIN ILONA IN AUSCHWITZ. I WAS SO HAPPY TO SEE HER, AND AT THE SAME TIME SO SAD THAT SHE WAS THERE.

I ASKED HER WHERE TOMIK WAS. SHE SHOOK HER HEAD.

TOMIK WAS DEAD.

WE WERE PUT ON A TRAIN AGAIN, HEADING TO TWO OR THREE CAMPS. AMONG THEM WAS ONE CALLED BRAUNSCHWEIG.

WHEN THE WAR ENDED, WE WERE SENT AWAY ON A TRAIN. THAT TRAIN WENT AROUND EUROPE FOR TEN DAYS AND STOPPED AT THE DANISH BORDER.

I THOUGHT I WAS GOING TO DIE ON THAT TRAIN. BUT I SURVIVED. THEY DIDN'T KNOW WHAT TO DO WITH US.

I WAS VERY ILL.

I DON'T KNOW EXACTLY HOW, BUT WE ARRIVED IN MALMOE, SWEDEN, AND AFTER THAT, IN A CITY CALLED VÄXJÖ. AND AFTER THAT, AT A SANATORIUM.

I WAS ALL ALONE WHEN I GOT TO SWEDEN.

AT THE SANATORIUM I WOULD LOOK OUT THE WINDOW AT THE PARK. I SAW A SIGN THAT SAID "FORBIDDEN." I THOUGHT IT SAID "FORBIDDEN FOR *JEWS*," SO I DIDN'T DARE GO OUTDOORS.

I THOUGHT IT WAS HAPPENING ALL OVER AGAIN. I DIDN'T UNDERSTAND THAT THE WAR WAS OVER.

AFTER THE SANATORIUM I WENT TO A REFUGEE CAMP OUTSIDE STOCKHOLM. I SAW SOME OLD FRIENDS AND MET BOYS AND GIRLS THAT, LIKE ME, HAD SURVIVED.

I STARTED TO FEEL AT HOME. WE BECAME A LITTLE FAMILY THAT STAYED TOGETHER. I STILL HAVE THOSE FRIENDS TODAY.

MY OLDER BROTHER EMERICH AND I DIDN'T KNOW WHERE EACH OTHER WERE FOR A WHOLE YEAR.

I WAITED FOR HIM TO COME BACK TO ME. DURING MY TIME IN SWEDEN I WROTE TO MY COUSIN IN PALESTINE, AND EMERICH WROTE TO HIM, TOO.

OUR COUSIN REALIZED THAT EACH OF US DIDN'T KNOW THAT THE OTHER HAD SURVIVED. HE CONNECTED US AND AFTER THAT EMERICH WROTE TO ME FROM ITALY WHERE HE WAS LIVING. IN 1949, I WENT TO SEE HIM.

I STAYED WITH HIM FOR TWO MONTHS. WE NEVER TALKED ABOUT THE PEOPLE WE LOST. WE NEVER TALKED ABOUT OUR MEMORIES.

FOR A SHORT WHILE IN MY LIFE I WAS HAPPY, AND I FORGOT EVERYTHING ABOUT THE HORRORS I HAD LIVED THROUGH.

EVERYONE CARRIES
THEIR LITTLE LUGGAGE.
THIS WAS MINE.

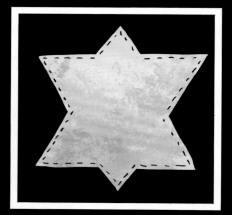

Elisabeth Masur says that there are no words to explain the things that she has been through. She has tried to live a normal life, but her experiences have followed her everywhere. Elisabeth has two children, as well as grandchildren and great grandchildren. She says that she has had many happy times throughout her life, but she has never felt like a whole person.

TIMELINE

January 30, 1933
Adolf Hitler, leader of the National Socialist German Workers Party, becomes head of the government in Germany.

1933-1935
The German Parliament successfully introduces laws that isolate Jews from the rest of society, limiting their freedom and opportunities.

September 15, 1935
The Nürnberg (or Nuremberg) Laws are announced in Germany. Jews no longer have rights as German citizens. Marriage and sexual intercourse between Jews and non-Jews is prohibited.

March 12, 1938
German troops enter Austria.

October 28, 1938
17,000 Jews of Polish descent are forced to leave Germany for Poland.

November 9-10, 1938
Kristallnacht (Crystal Night): Jews are hunted and murdered, their property is destroyed, and synagogues are burned down all over Germany.

March 15, 1939
Germany invades Czechoslovakia.

September 1, 1939
Germany attacks Poland and World War II breaks out. The day after, Italy announces an alliance with Germany. Great Britain and France declare war against Germany on September 3. The Swedish government announces neutrality in the ongoing war.

September 17, 1939
The Soviet Union invades Poland from the east.

September 21, 1939
In Poland, Jews are transferred by force to specific areas called ghettos.

December 1, 1939
All Jews living in Poland must carry the Star of David visibly on their person. Later, that will include all Jews in Germany and in German-occupied territories.

1940
Germany invades Norway and Denmark. Sweden allows Germany to transport soldiers and weapons to and from Norway through Sweden. German troops invade Belgium, the Netherlands, and Luxembourg. They continue onto France and occupy Paris.

German troops attack Britain. Large parts of London are destroyed by German bombings.

June 21, 1941
Germany attacks the Soviet Union.

December 7, 1941
The Japanese air force attacks the United States Naval Base at Pearl Harbor. Together with their Allies, the U.S. declares war against Japan, Germany, and Italy.

1941-1942
Six extermination camps are established in Poland by the Germans. Among them is Auschwitz-Birkenau.

January 20, 1942
German officers gather outside Berlin for the Wannsee Conference, to discuss the "Final Solution" for the "Jewish issue." The plan: to systematically exterminate the Jewish people. 74,000 Jews are sent to extermination camps.

1942-1943
German troops deport Jews from ghettos to camps. Thousands are put to death in gas chambers and through forced labor.

February 2, 1943
Soviet troops defeat the German army at Stalingrad (today Volograd).

April 19, 1943
The Warsaw Rising breaks out against German troops, the largest resistance in occupied Europe, with a significant symbolic impact.

October 1943
Sweden welcomes Danish Jews, a vast majority of which reach Sweden by boat.

March 19, 1944
Germany invades Hungary. Soon Jews are deported to Poland.

June 6, 1944
D-Day: Western Allied forces successfully march on Normandy, France. The troops continue fighting Nazi forces throughout Europe.

1944
The Soviet Union attacks German forces in Eastern Europe and makes their way through Poland where they discover several concentration camps.

Year's end, 1944-45
German forces in Poland escape the Soviet army, forcing more than 100,000 prisoners from the camps to follow, often by foot, back to Germany. Later this is called the March of Death, because of the large number of prisoners that died of exhaustion or were shot to death along the way.

1945
The Allies continue making their way through Europe, to Germany, discovering camps filled with prisoners, many so weak they die during liberation. Survivors reach Sweden with the White Buses, a Swedish rescue action coordinated by the Red Cross. Sweden welcomes 10,000 refugees to be rehabilitated at hospitals and refugee camps throughout the country.

January 27, 1945
The Soviet army liberates the prisoners, mostly sick or dying, in the Auschwitz camps. In 2005, the United Nations declares January 27 International Holocaust Remembrance Day.

April 30, 1945
Adolf Hitler commits suicide.

May 7-8, 1945
Germany surrenders. The war is over in Europe.

July 17-August 2, 1945
The Allied powers disarm Germany, their war industries are destroyed, and those responsible for the crimes against humanity stand for an international military court of law. Germany is divided into four zones of occupation controlled by Britain, the U.S., France, and the Soviet Union.

Summer 1945
Throughout Europe, refugee camps are established to help prisoners and survivors of the Holocaust. Slowly, survivors find their way back into everyday life. Bureaus are established to help people find family and friends that also survived, and to help re-establish their lives.

August 1945
The U.S. drops nuclear bombs on Hiroshima and Nagasaki in Japan. Hundreds of thousands are killed, and Japan surrenders. World War II comes to an end.

October 24, 1945
The United Nations is formed and its statutes adopted.

November 20, 1945
An international trial in Nürnberg (Nuremberg) against the German war criminals commences. Other trials follow.

GLOSSARY

Allies: Military alliance during World War II between nations united against Germany, Italy, and Japan. The Allied nations included France, Poland, the United Kingdom, and later the Soviet Union, the United States, and China.

Antisemitism: Prejudices and hostility against Jewish people.

Concentration camps: Camps where prisoners were forced to labor and kept locked away, because of their political views, religion, ethnic background, sexual orientation, or criminality.

Crystal Night (Kristallnacht): Persecution of Jews on the nights of November 9-10, 1938. Many Jews were murdered, thousands were arrested, and their homes, businesses, and synagogues were destroyed.

Deport: To expel or forcefully transfer people from one area to another.

Disinfect: To clean material or humans using chemicals so that infectious agents or diseases are not transmitted.

Extermination camps: Camps with the purpose of committing mass murder, primarily through gas chambers. During World War II, the Nazi Germans created six extermination camps in Poland where mostly Jews, but also Romanians and other groups, were murdered.

Gas chamber: Rooms in some extermination camps where the Nazis committed mass murder using exhaust from cars or poisoned gas.

Ghetto: During World War II, ghettos were used for creating isolated and restricted living areas for Jews. Romanians were also sometimes placed there.

Hitler, Adolf (1889-1945): Leader of the National Socialist German Workers Party and political leader of Germany from 1934-1945.

Holocaust: The Nazi genocide of Jews, Romanians, the disabled, and dissidents.

March of Death: Marches that prisoners were forced to walk as the SS emptied all concentration camps, because the Allies were closing in on them in 1945. A large number of the prisoners died from starvation, exhaustion, or were shot to death.

Mengele, Josef (1911-1979): Chief Doctor in the concentration camp in Auschwitz. He performed reckless experiments on the prisoners, and selected which Jews would go straight to the gas chambers when arriving to Auschwitz.

National Socialist German Workers Party: German Political Party from 1920 to 1945. Also called the Nazi Party. A German political movement with an anti-democratic ideology. The Nazis wanted to create a German fellowship that did not include Jews, Romanians, homosexuals, dissidents, or disabled people.

Occupation: When one country takes over a place or a group of people in another country by force.

Rationing cards/tickets: Coupons to buy things like food when supplies grow scarce during war.

SS: The Schutzstaffel, or Protection Squad, a Nazi military organization in Germany during the years of 1925-1945. They started off as body guards for Adolf Hitler, but quickly expanded their power, promoting the Nazi ideology and supervising the extermination of the Jews.

Star of David: Jewish symbol, a six-pointed star. From 1935 and onwards, Nazis forced Jews to wear a yellow star of David on their clothes.

Surrender: To give up in a conflict.

Swastika: Symbol for the National Socialist German Workers Party; in 1933, it became the official symbol of the German realms.

Synagogue: Jewish congregation hall for services.

Tuberculosis: Disease in which the lungs are attacked by bacteria; curable with penicillin and other medical treatment.

Typhus: A common disease during World War II among soldiers and in ghettos and in camps. Deadly if not treated.

United Nations (UN): Created by the Allies as World War II ended, founded to work for international peace. Almost every country in the world now has members in the UN.

White busses: A mission by the Red Cross to transport survivors of camps at the end of the war, to Sweden and other places.

Yiddish: Language spoken by the majority of Jews in central and eastern Europe before World War II.

DO YOU WANT TO LEARN MORE?

This book is inspired by *Survivors of the Holocaust* by Kate Schackelton, Zane Whittingham, and Ryan Jones, published by The Watts Publishing group.

Some of the information in this book is taken from Living History Forum and the Swedish Antisemitism Committee. Visit their home pages to learn more:

www.levandehistoria.se
www.skma.se

And in the United States:
https://aboutholocaust.org/about/

SPECIAL THANKS

Tobias Rawet
Livia Fränkel
Selma Bengtsson
Susanna Christensen
Emerich Roth
Elisabeth Masur

For having the strength to tell those of us who were not there about your experiences, so that we can tell it to the generations that come after us.

Thank you to the Swedish Committee Against Antisemitism, the Living History Forum, the Association of Holocaust Survivors in Sweden, and the Order of the Teaspoon, for your missions to inform, educate, and explore with future generations how they can make better decisions, be brave, and make the world a better place.

Thank you, Jonna Wolff.

Thank you, Suzanne Kaplan.

Thank you, Ingrid Lomfors.

Thank you, Marie, for giving me this opportunity, and to Peter, for giving these stories life.

Thank you, Kerstin, for making this understandable.

—JBB

To Scott Allie for making me a better artist.
Without your feedback over the years this book simply
wouldn't have been possible.

To all the folks at Dark Horse Comics
for crafting this edition. You rock, as always!

To Mike Mignola.
Your style influenced this even more than
our recent collaborations.

To Chris Golden for allowing me to hone
my craft together with a great writer over so many books.

To Katii O'Brien and Jenny Blenk
for the continued heartfelt feedback on my art.

To Marie Augustsson and Jessica Bab Bonde
for picking me as artist for this book.

To our team at Natur och Kultur
who crafted the Swedish edition.

And to all of the survivors,
for allowing me to be a small part of your story.
Your voices will live with me forever.

—PB

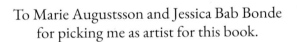

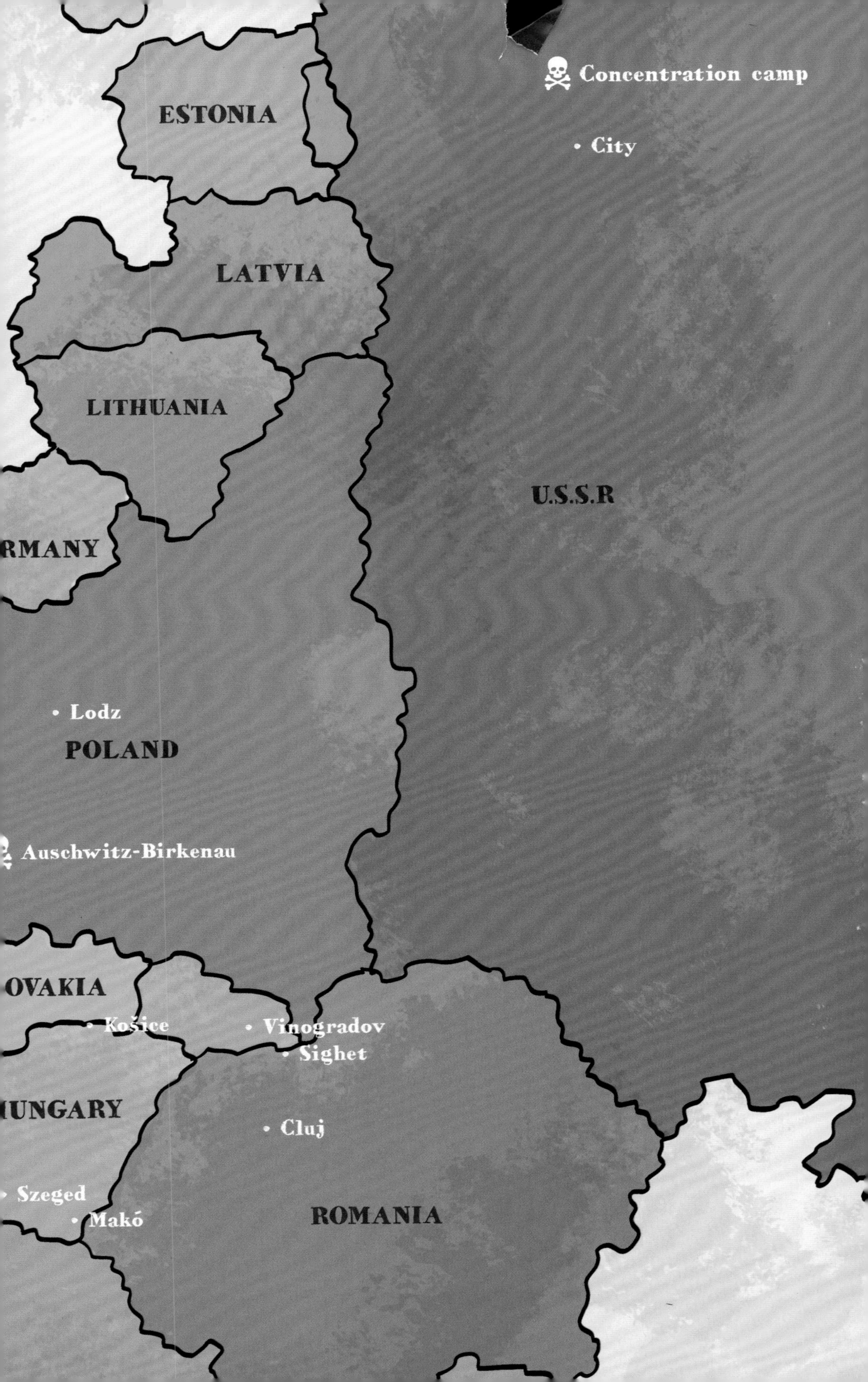
Concentration camp
City
ESTONIA
LATVIA
LITHUANIA
RMANY
U.S.S.R
Lodz
POLAND
Auschwitz-Birkenau
OVAKIA
Košice
Vinogradov
Sighet
HUNGARY
Cluj
Szeged
Makó
ROMANIA

ALSO FROM DARK HORSE BOOKS

Joe Golem Occult Detective Volume 3: The Drowning City

By Mike Mignola, Christopher Golden, Peter Bergting & Michelle Madsen

A chilling new adventure unfolds as Joe Golem investigates the kidnapping of a conjuror and the strange men who took him. Aided by the victim's ward, a spunky teenage girl, the detective soon finds that otherworldly forces are at work. The only way to stop the madman behind the kidnapping and occult activities is to locate a strange object known as Lector's Pentajulum. But how can they locate it, who else is trying to track it down, and how can it save both them and the city?
Hardcover, $24.99
ISBN 978-1-50670-945-1

Baltimore Volume 5: The Apostle and the Witch of Harju

By Mike Mignola, Christopher Golden, Peter Bergting, Ben Stenbeck & Dave Stewart

Lord Baltimore hunts the godlike Red King, who is responsible for the vampire plague. After saving a young woman from her undead husband, Baltimore and his team of fearless vampire killers face the demonic offspring of a witch and uncover the truth about the inquisitor-turned-werewolf Judge Duvic—now more bloodthirsty than ever.
Hardcover, $24.99
ISBN 978-1-61655-618-1

The Dark North

By Peter Bergting, Martin Dunelind, Henrik Pettersson, Joakim Ericsson, Magnus Olsson & Lukas Thelin

Originally crowdfunded in 2015, this illustrated prose/art book fusion features five unique tales ranging from Norse mythology to science fiction, showcasing artwork by Scandinavia's leading illustrators and concept artists and a foreword by author and filmmaker Clive Barker!
Hardcover, $34.99
ISBN 978-1-50670-467-8

Two Brothers

By Gabriel Bá & Fábio Moon

Family secrets engage the reader in this profoundly resonant story about identity, love, loss, deception, and the dissolution of blood ties. Based on the novel by Milton Hatoum.
Hardcover, $24.99
ISBN 978-1-61655-856-7

Avatar the Last Airbender: Team Avatar Tales

By Gene Luen Yang, Faith Erin Hicks, Carla Speed McNeil & Others

Journey along with Team Avatar as they rescue a pumpkin farmer waylaid by monsters, help an old rival with a hair-raising problem, and reflect on what it means to save the world.
Trade paperback, $10.99
ISBN 978-1-50670-793-8

The Girl in the Bay

By J.M. DeMatteis & Corin Howell

In 1969, seventeen-year-old Kathy Sartori is brutally attacked, her body hurled into Brooklyn's Sheepshead Bay. Miraculously, she survives, fights her way back to the surface, only to discover that fifty years have passed, and an eerie doppelganger has lived out an entire life in her place. Kathy soon confronts not just this strange double, but the madman who "murdered" her five decades earlier.
Trade paperback, $17.99
ISBN 978-1-50671-228-4

Fax from Sarajevo

By Joe Kubert

Legendary comics artist Joe Kubert tells the heartbreaking story of the Serbian attack of Bosnia and Herzegovina in the early 1990s, based on faxes sent by Kubert's agent Ervin Rustemagić while he and his family spent two years trapped in the city under siege. The booked was named the best graphic novel of 1996 by the Washington Times and won numbers of comics industry awards in the U.S. and abroad.
Trade paperback, $19.99
ISBN 978-1-50671-663-3

Black Hammer '45: From the World of Black Hammer

By Jeff Lemire, Ray Fawkes & Matt Kindt

During the Golden Age of superheroes, an elite Air Force crew called the Black Hammer Squadron bands together to combat the Nazis, a host of occult threats, and their ultimate aerial warrior the Ghost Hunter.
Trade paperback, $17.99
ISBN 978-1-50670-850-8

Stranger Things Volume 1: The Other Side

By Jody Houser & Stefano Martino

When Will Byers finds himself in the Upside Down, an impossible dark parody of his own world, he's understandably frightened. But that's nothing compared with the fear that takes hold when he realizes what's in that world with him!
Trade paperback, $17.99
ISBN 978-1-50670-976-5

Umbrella Academy Volume 1: Apocalypse Suite

By Gerard Way & Gabriel Bá

Forty-three extraordinary children were spontaneously born by women who'd previously shown no signs of pregnancy. Millionaire inventor Reginald Hargreeves adopted seven of the children; when asked why, his only explanation was, "To save the world."
Trade paperback, $17.99
ISBN 978-1-59307-978-9

AVAILABLE AT YOUR LOCAL COMICS SHOP OR BOOKSTORE
TO FIND A COMICS SHOP IN YOUR AREA, VISIT COMICSHOPLOCATOR.COM
For more information or to order direct, visit DarkHorse.com

DarkHorse.com

Joe Golem: Occult Detective™ & © 2012 Mike Mignola, Christopher Golden. Baltimore™ & © 2007 Mike Mignola, Christopher Golden. Text and illustrations of The Dark North™ © 2016 Charles Wood Publishing AB. Two Brothers © Fábio Moon and Gabriel Bá. "Dois Irmãos" original text © 2000 Milton Hatoum. Adaptation and illustrations © 2015 Fábio Moon and Gabriel Bá. Nickelodeon Avatar: The Last Airbender™ & © 2019 Viacom International, Inc. All rights reserved. Nickelodeon, Nickelodeon Avatar: The Last Airbender, and all related titles, logos, and characters are trademarks of Viacom International, Inc. Text and illustrations of The Girl in the Bay™ & © 2019 J.M. DeMatteis and Corin Howell. Fax from Sarajevo © 2018 Strip Art Features, www.safcomics.com. Black Hammer™ & © 2019 171 Studios, Inc., and Dean Ormston. Black Hammer and all characters prominently featured herein are trademarks of 171 Studios, Inc., and Dean Ormston. Stranger Things™ & © 2019 Netflix. Umbrella Academy™ & © 2008, 2020 Gerard Way and Gabriel Bá. Dark Horse Books® and the Dark Horse logo are registered trademarks of Dark Horse Comics, Inc. All rights reserved.